ADVANCE PRAISE FOR STARSTRUCK

"What can a radish teach us about humanity? More than you'd think. Filled with beautiful prose, vibrant characters, and heart-stirring reflections on the sacrifice of self for love, this is a book that will give you ALL THE FEELS. I got withdrawal symptoms every time I put it down."
— Robyn Bennis, author of the Signal Airship series

"Oh what a song for living this book is. Brimming with warmth, Startruck is a story about lost souls coming together, loving each other despite their circumstances, suspicions, and newness. Ogden is masterful in creating a group of characters–a radish, a fox, a heap of rocks, and a lost boy– that you would go to the ends of the universe for. It's a breathtakingly human story, and every emotion is raw and to the fore. If you're searching for a book that hits those Studio Ghibli vibes just right, this should be your next read."
— Lyndsie Manusos, author of *From These Dark Abodes*

"Starstruck is filled with whimsy and tenderness, and populated by odd and endearing characters with whom we become fast friends. But it's also filled with heavy truths about growing older, painful family secrets, and the perils of a changing world. I could feel the cracks forming in my heart with every page turn. What a strange and lovely book."
— Josh Rountree, author of *The Legend of Charlie Fish*

"Aimee Ogden has done it again! Deliciously strange and heartbreakingly sweet, Starstruck will have you rooting for a lovable cast of characters the likes of which you've never seen before. Ogden's work is always full of surprising delights, and this is no exception."
— Samantha Mills, award-winning author of *The Wings Upon Her Back*

STARSTRUCK

Aimee Ogden

FOR ROBYN.
SHE KNOWS WHAT SHE DID.

Prish had always been the kind of radish who knew what she was about. Maybe that was why she hadn't noticed sooner that Alsing had grown pensive and quiet in the evenings, that she took longer than usual washing up the dinner dishes or with the mending. Prish had never minded long silences; a thoughtful pause could cultivate all manner of interesting things. Plants like herself tended to have more patience than animals. Their lives-before, rooted to the ground and always waiting for a glimpse of sun, required such a temperament. So, out in the sprawling gardens behind their cabin, with the friendly pat of rhubarb leaves on her shoulders and the idle conversation of bumblebees in her ears, it was too easy to miss the things that didn't get said, the hopes that got silently dashed, the neighborly visits that slowly dried up.

She'd noticed, of course, that no stars had fallen for a while. Hard to miss that their little cabin deep in the wood hadn't welcomed any newly starstruck guests. The last such had been an elderly squirrel, his dark eyes suspicious of Alsing—a fox, herself—as she offered him clothes to fit his newly human-like form (she had long experience sewing trousers with a comfortable hole in the place where a tail should emerge). He'd stayed with them for two weeks, until his two-legged tottering grew steady and confident, until he had learned his way around cutlery and shirt-buttons and even (briefly and not entirely successfully) Alsing's bicycle. Then they'd waved him off as he set out for the city, glancing back toward the cabin on every fourth or fifth step.

And not a soul since. They still sat out on the cabin's little porch each evening, with cups of iced tea in the summer and steaming mugs of mulled wine in winter, and watched the skies. Sometimes a star would streak across the sky, but it always disappeared somewhere far behind the horizon, without the telltale flare of light to herald a new-made starstruck's arrival in the world. "Looks like another quiet night," Prish would say, when her eyes grew weary and her long leafy hair wilted for want of sleep. She and Alsing hadn't yet lived in here the cabin long enough to have grown old together, but they weren't young anymore, either. "Maybe tomorrow."

"Maybe tomorrow," Alsing always agreed, and it was easy enough not to worry about the extra time she took gathering herself up out of the rocking chair, the restless flick of her ears. She was forever flicking her ears, anyway, when she hadn't yet had her morning cup of coffee or when Prish tracked dirt from the gardens into the kitchen or when she got too busy after that morning cup of coffee to take just one blasted minute to visit the outhouse, for goodness' sake.

So one evening, in the early autumn, when Prish draped a faded quilt over her wife's shoulders and kissed her cheek and invited her out to the porch, she was taken aback when Alsing said *no*, and burst into smothered, hiccupping sobs.

Prish maneuvered Alsing to the sofa, the same one that she'd found on the side of the street in the city twenty years ago, before they'd met. Alsing had sewn slipcovers for the arms of the sofa, to hide the worn spots and a worrying stain, and she picked at one of these now with the tip of one claw. Tea was made. Hugs were offered. A clean handkerchief was procured, and then, a second.

"It's your *starday*," she told Prish, with another damp honk into the much-abused handkerchief.

Prish filed this information away thoughtlessly in the coat pockets of her mind, where it would slip out again sooner or later when she rooted around there for the symptoms of grot-root in tomatoes or the last place she'd seen the farmer's almanac. She marked Alsing's starday yearly with alacrity, and with a massive bouquet of all their favorite flowers (it helped that Alsing's starday fell at the end of May). Celebrating Prish's own starday had never offered her much interest; to her it had always been a day like any other, and she'd long discouraged Alsing from making her desired fuss about it. And anyway, during the harvest season, there was plenty else to do, in the gardens and in the kitchen, besides nibble on cake; every other weekend she also hitched the cart to the back of a bicycle to take their extra provisions into the city of Eltomel, to deliver to the regular customers with whom they had arrangements.

Besides, her original starday hadn't been that much of an event to begin with. Certainly nothing as traumatic or dramatic as Alsing's. There had been a flash of light, accompanied by a flash of existence, and she'd pulled herself the rest of the way out of the soil of a small farm in the Lowland Downs. Starstruck ages didn't match up exactly to those of their human counterparts, but she would have been a young woman, built stout and sturdy in a human-like shape with knotted, twisted stems and roots in place of flesh, with clumps of dirt still clinging to the tiny hairs on her arms and legs and feet. She'd gone up to the farmhouse and knocked on the door, where a human farmer had emerged in a nightshirt and a pair of muddy boots. He'd studied her for a moment and then yawned enormously. "Martha Ann!" he'd called over his shoulder, without quite waiting for the yawn to wrap up. "One of the watermelon radishes went and got starstruck. Fetch me down a pair of your old overalls, will you?"

And so Prish had been dressed, been cooked a midnight dinner of scrambled eggs and uncured bacon, and then been shooed off to sleep on a pile of old quilts by the old man and his daughter. When Prish woke up in the morning, the farmer handed her a basket and asked how she felt about chickens. She hadn't been sure, just then, but she'd been willing to find out. (Chickens were perfectly fine, it turned out. She would have liked to keep a henhouse at the cabin, too, but Alsing said the temptation was too great.)

Waiting for Alsing to elaborate on the importance of her starday proved fruitless. Prish stroked the back of her hand, careful to follow the grain of the fur. "I'm not sure I understand, Whiskers. I don't *think* you're upset that I was starstruck in the first place?"

"Well, of course not!" Annoyance displaced some of the sadness in Alsing's voice. She sat up a little straighter on the sofa and kicked Prish lightly in the shin. "Don't be ridiculous, you mean old thing." She delivered one last final-sounding blow into the handkerchief and set it aside. "It's just that it marks a different anniversary, too.

Haven't you been counting? It's been eighteen months. A year and a half." Her head turned toward the little window that let out onto the porch. "Since the last star fell."

Prish snorted. "It can't have been that long already! Why, old Vendiero was just here in the spring, and..." She trailed off, doing the mental accounting. Not this spring, was it? This spring they'd used the little guest room as a storage space after an April storm took the roof off the shed. She felt her mouth open and close a few times, but nothing came out and nothing went in, not agreement or apologies or air. "Someone would have mentioned," she insisted stubbornly. But who? They hardly ever saw their neighbors here, as far apart as they were all spread in the Craftwood, and when she went into the city, she kept her head down and made her deliveries and came swiftly back home.

"I know. I know. You do lose track of the time, dear heart." Now it was Alsing's turn to turn their hands over, so that hers lay on top of Prish's, giving back some of the comfort she'd so recently taken. "But it has been a long, long time."

"But surely somewhere else—" Prish cut herself off again. Even in Eltomel, she couldn't remember the last time someone had ushered forward a hesitant new starstruck to meet her. *Someone* would have said something to her, wouldn't they? But maybe it was too strange a subject to broach. Or maybe there had been gossip that Prish had missed: half-heard conversations, idle chatter.

She couldn't make it make sense. They'd *seen* lights in the sky, over the last year and more. Just because none of the starstruck had arrived on their doorstep didn't mean they hadn't arrived anywhere at all. "They must be falling *somewhere*," she insisted stubbornly.

They both sat with that hollow insistence for a moment, waiting for a fresh idea to breathe new life into it. Waiting for it to swell with real hope. But nothing came. Like the stars, it seemed, hope had somewhere better to be. If the stars were falling, they were falling too far away for them to know about it. Too far away for lonely starstruck to find their way into Eltomel to meet her.

It was too much to contemplate what might have stoppered up the stars; what it meant that the world would be deprived of any more beings as wonderful as Alsing ever again. Prish had always been the kind of radish who knew what she was about, and what she was about fell comfortably within the fences of her garden and the walls of her house and the confines of her heart. What she had always been about, really, was Alsing.

Alsing held out the quilt to one side, and Prish squeezed in alongside her, her chin resting on Alsing's shoulder, Alsing's ear flicking restlessly against the top of her head.

There was nothing else to do then but to ask it, the only question she could think of, the one whose answer she already knew and had to hear anyway.

"What do you want to do now?" she said.

"I..." Alsing's ears stilled, flattening along the back of her head. "I don't want to be here anymore."

Prish marshaled arguments she knew would never see combat: the garden bed she'd just tucked in for a winter slumber under a thick blanket of compost, and the stalks still waiting for the first frost before they offered up one last harvest of sweet, plump sprouts. The raspberry jungle she'd coaxed out of a few recalcitrant canes, and the bench built for two on the back porch, and the three apple trees she'd planted last year that she would never see bear fruit. The last pumpkins, still green and unfulfilled on the vine.

"Well then," Prish said briskly, sending her disappointment and disagreement to an unearned early retirement. "It only makes sense for us to go."

✦

It took a few days to sort through all their things, choosing what could go with them to Eltomel, what must stay, what they were in fact relieved to unburden themselves of. In the end, they had their two little suitcases stuffed with clothes, a steamer trunk of dubious quality full of household goods too beloved to part with, a basket of Alsing's finished mending-work that would need to be returned to its city-folk owners, and a few apple boxes they packed with jars of jam and the last of the carrots and apples from the trees that had so long sheltered Prish's gardens. It was an unbearably small collection to represent all the years they'd spent together here, but it was what would fit on the cart behind the bicycle, so that was that.

As apple trees themselves were not so readily packed up into boxes, Prish spent one quiet hour sitting beneath her favorite of the little orchard, a friendly stooped old thing. If a little sap escaped her eyes, she made sure it was dry before she went back inside.

They made love one last time in the old creaky bed, the intertwined roots between Prish's legs softening, separating, to admit gentle fingers and carefully trimmed claws. Starstruck bodies were in many ways like human bodies—Alsing's more than Prish's—so that they could talk and eat and screw and sing. It was simply that they did so more or less *differently* than a human body would have done. Prish had no blood and no lungs and no proper guts and no bones. There was no reason she should have been able to experience sensations of the sexual variety, let alone whisper her wife's name against her ear, or see the tip of her perfect black nose out of the corner of her eye. The only answer any doctor or scientist could give for how it all worked was "magic." And it certainly felt like magic, didn't it, to be held like this, and to love like that?

Once the heights of ecstasy had fallen away beneath her, Prish found herself breathing hard and fast, waiting for sweet reason to return to her thick radish head. The pale green loops of stem around her torso had gone somewhat slack, and between them, glimmers of gold light could be seen: her star, locked away inside her chest—no bigger than a marble, yet filled, somehow, with everything that made her Prish, a radish with a name and a favorite person and any number of bad habits.

"Put that away," said Alsing teasingly, and pretended to cover the star with the palm of her paw. "Positively indecent." Somewhere behind her own fur and flesh and bone, beside her own beating heart, the same sort of star shone with hidden light. She said, turning the page of her mood to a more serious chapter: "You'll hold me, won't you, until I fall asleep?"

"I'll hold you to the end of the world," Prish promised, "and farther. If you're willing to stay married to me after a trip like that."

They curled up together, heads and shoulders and hips turning this way and that until a comfortable compromise of position could be achieved. Though she never succeeded, Prish tried as she always did to stay awake until Alsing fell asleep. This time, as ever, her whirling thoughts weren't enough to keep her eyes open—they only spun her around and around into a quick, dizzy slumber.

When she dreamed, she dreamed of the old farmer's fields and the patchwork night sky over Eltomel, where the streetlamps held back the full weight of the dark. It was she who woke first, as was also usually her custom, with Alsing's warm breath on her shoulder. She moved away from its whiskery tickle against her flesh but couldn't go far with Alsing's head on her arm. She sighed.

It had been a long time since she'd really studied the beams of the ceiling over the bed; the way the dawnlight broke in through the dusty window. She understood why Alsing couldn't bear to be here any longer—but she also didn't want to go. Eltomel was somewhere else, and it was, at least, familiar; or it had been once. But right now, she felt that there wasn't any place that would ever be fully theirs, fully right, for them. *This* had been that place, here in between the lumpy mattress and the dust-fogged window; but this place had stopped existing to Alsing, now that the skies had dried up.

Perhaps distance would make it stop existing for Prish, too.

Her arm had started to tingle; she adjusted it minutely beneath Alsing's neck without disturbing her. You couldn't belong somewhere, she thought, not really and not forever. But you could belong to some*one*, and she should count herself fortunate to have found just such a person. She would do anything for that person, if she asked it. Or if she *didn't* ask. There were worse things to lose than a place, however dear.

Eltomel wasn't so far, all things considered. And Prish always did her best to consider every last thing.

———◆———

It was already bound to be a longer trip than usual into Eltomel, seeing as the bicycle only had one seat and neither of them were young enough anymore to find riding on the handlebars a pleasant prospect. They took turns riding and walking, and Prish was hard pressed to decide which activity was worse: plodding along on foot or pushing hard through the pedals to keep the cart in inertia's thrall.

But Alsing had also asked not to head straight to the city. They had neighbors—if you could call someone who lived miles away and who you saw once every month or two a "neighbor"—to whom she wished to say goodbye. "We can stay with the Midderwells the first night," Alsing said, "or, if they're less hospitable than usual, in Jaffen Anderbee's barn and he'll be none the wiser."

The prospect of sleeping on a dirt floor sent a preemptive jolt of dismay through Prish's back and hips. (No bones, no joints, yet she still managed to wake up in an achy knot as often as not.) But she only said, "Then that's what we'll do, Whiskers." And Alsing's glad little, sad little smile made up for quite a lot of future aches and pains.

But as chance would have it, they would not spend that night under the Midderwells' roof, nor under old Anderbee's straw-pile. They were moving even slower than Prish had figured on, and their goodbyes with Widow Sonyella endured even longer than Alsing had imagined, and a chilly dusk was already folding itself in around them when they were still some two hours' walk from either neighbor's fence. "Oh dear, oh dear," muttered Alsing repeatedly. Her limp had begun to come out the longer they were on the road, and Prish wasn't sure if she was having the worst of it from the pain or from the sense that she was responsible for the delay.

That latter was nonsense; Prish could have hastened their parting with poor old Sonyella at any point, or put her foot down altogether and said *no thank you very much* to the prospect of this final round of neighborly visitations, so really it was she who ought to be held to account, and she said as much, and Alsing said that this little farewell tour had been her desire in the first place and it was she who ought to have done a better job managing it and that was nothing to do with Prish, and Prish had begged her pardon and noted that they were partners after all and that she would like to think she had everything to do with it actually, and Alsing said that of course she hadn't meant it like *that*, and then a streak of light screamed across the sky and smashed into the treetops with a triumphant thunderclap, not a hundred yards from where they stood.

They stared after it for a long silent while. Alsing's mouth hung loosely open, while Prish found hers pressed closed, the thick green-white skin of her face curling tightly inward as if to protect the pink flesh inside. "How *did* you mean it, then?" she said, retreating to their exceptionally silly argument just to have a track to set her thoughts on and see if she couldn't get them rolling forward again.

Her thoughts failed to cooperate, but the question did get Alsing moving. She spun to Prish, a thousand emotions knotted together in her face and impossible to untangle, but hope was the loom that held the whole thing together. "Come on," she said. Her claws brushed Prish's coat jacket. "Leave the bike for now. Let's go and meet them, dear heart."

They left the bike behind a cluster of bushes beside the path and raced off through the wood, struggling through the waist-high bushes and the grabby little fingers of choke-vines. Who would it be, waiting, bewildered, with the new weight of a star inside them? A squirrel, an owl, a muskrat? Maybe even a fellow plant, a wild cousin of the woods to Prish, an autumn aster or even an oak tree with late-year gold in their tumbled leaf-hair. She'd never been the kind of radish who carried her hope around with her, not like Alsing did, but she felt a stir of excitement that surprised and pleased her.

"Here," said Alsing, breathless, limping worse than ever now. "I think it's just through here—"

They stumbled together into a clearing, where Alsing stopped so suddenly that Prish smashed into her back and sent them both tumbling. "Oh, skies above, Alsing!" she gasped, rolling to the side and looking her wife over for scratches or scrapes. "What in the heavens possessed you to—"

But when she looked up at the dark shape looming over them both, it became immediately apparent what had possessed Alsing, and it possessed Prish, too, knocking all the wind from her body and the thoughts from her head.

"Well, good evening," said the starstruck...person. Its body was both more humanlike than Alsing's or Prish's, and less. It could have been carved by a sculptor with a tender eye for detail: the gentle point of an elbow, a round belly, five dexterous fingers on each hand and five wiggling toes on each foot. Between its legs, it was smooth and sexless, and its whole body could have been carved from a single seamless pillar of stone. And its face—sweet skies! It had no face at all, only a rough, rocky surface on the gray basalt stone that formed its head. The bottom narrowed to a lopsided point that suggested a chin and widened from there to an uneven triangle at the top. Faceless and eyeless as it was, Prish felt its gaze on her and disliked the feeling immensely. *Magic,* yes, of course. But living stone? How could it be? She'd never heard of the like. "It's lovely to meet you both." The stone head canted to one side in puzzlement. "Or at least I think it is. I've never met anyone else before, so I have to assume. It *is* nice to meet you, isn't it?"

"Very nice indeed," said Alsing, who struggled to her feet with Prish's assistance. All the dismay that Prish felt, looking at this impossible being, was transmuted in Alsing to pure wonderment. "And very unusual. You're...may I?" The starstruck stone bent forward to meet Alsing's curious reaching fingers. She ran her hand across the sheer plane of the stone's face. "There's never been a starstruck stone before, not that I've heard in all my life."

"Oh, that makes sense." The stone examined its own hands, turning them this way and that, flexing the fingers. "I had a suspicion I might be rather special. I suppose I'm destined for great things!"

In the language of the long-married, Prish cast a sidelong glance at Alsing. In the same familiar tongue, Alsing gave Prish's sleeve a soft but firm pat. "Do you know your name yet, little one?"

"Oh, of course," said the starstruck stone, with great conviction, and sketched out a dainty curtsy. "Presenting, at her debut in the world of the animated and alive: Otra. How do you do?"

Because Otra had arrived in the world, as all starstruck did, entirely in the nude, Alsing promised her her pick of the extra clothing they'd packed. "Though some of them have a big hole in the seat area, mind," she added. "But I can sew that up for you easily enough, if we can stop somewhere with good enough light."

This sudden expansion of the meaning of the word *we* settled like an itch under Prish's skin. It was one thing to invite a stranger into the cabin, where she could retreat at will into her and Alsing's bedroom, or out into the gardens. She didn't even know, now, where Alsing meant to go next—continue on to the Anderbees' house, and from there to Eltomel? Go back home and set their eyes back on the stars?—and discussing it in Otra's presence unsettled her. Their ambiguous future meant that *we* would continue to be fifty percent larger for an unknown length of time. More, if you measured by mass.

A quiet trip with only her wife for company would have been one thing. This was something else entirely. Change was difficult enough, Prish felt, without having to put on a noble face about it in front of a stranger, and one who'd only just burst into existence at that.

Not that Otra's comportment was at all usual for a newly minted starstruck. She strolled self-assuredly through the woods, detailing her plans for fulfilling the important destiny she felt had been laid before her. "If I try to be in as many places as I can," she said cheerfully, "that increases the odds I'll be in the right place at the right time. Perhaps I could even try being in more than one place at once!"

"And how on earth do you propose to do that?" Prish couldn't help but ask, in spite of a valiant internal effort toward helping just that. She wilted under a sideways glance from Alsing.

"Oh, what a good question!" Otra fiddled with her own fingers, a mannerism that Prish found both distracting and tedious, and walked into a tree branch. "Oof! Well. I suppose I could invent time travel, or a self-duplication ray, or maybe I'm like earthworms and if you break me in half both of me will get up and wriggle away—"

"There will be no breaking anyone in half, please," said Alsing hastily, as Prish's head swam with the nightmare vision of *two* chattering Otras to tag along. "One place at a time will do just fine for the foreseeable future, I think. Oh, turn left here, little one, and we'll be back on the path, do you see?"

Otra, who had decided to lead the way despite having no idea where exactly Prish and Alsing had come from, swerved in the direction Alsing indicated. They emerged onto the path and in short order found the likely-looking cluster of bushes where they'd left the bicycle. Alsing offered Otra the suitcases, which she promptly upended. After a few minutes of cheerful rooting around, trying things on and tossing them aside, Otra settled on one of Alsing's blouses, a bit too frilly for frequent wear, with orange-gold embroidery on the collar and cuffs, and a pair of purplish wool trousers that belonged to Prish. The clothes fit snugly, but they did, fortunately, fit. Shoes, on the other hand, proved to be something of an issue; Alsing's delicate paws were far too small, and Prish's spare pair of clunky work boots were much bigger than Otra's stony feet. "She could just go barefoot," Prish suggested. "It's not as if rough terrain is going to hurt her, after all. It's made of the same stuff she is."

Otra drew up to her full height, pressing one hand to her button-front shirt in offense. "Nonsense! I can't very well go running around the forest in my bare feet like some kind of foundling child."

It seemed to Prish that some kind (and she wouldn't say *what* kind, exactly) of foundling child was exactly what Otra was. But under an apologetic glance from Alsing, she stuffed a rolled-up extra sock into the toe of each boot and helped Otra lace them up tightly.

"Perfect!" Otra proclaimed, and immediately set to work unlacing the boots again. "They will serve beautifully to carry me onward to destiny. First thing in the morning."

"She's right, dear heart," Alsing said, forestalling an instinctive objection. "It's already almost too dark to move on safely. We'll stay here for the night—just off the road." A flicker of a smile warmed her face. "Not that there's much in the way of brigands and highway robbers in these parts, but better safe than sorry, isn't it? And tomorrow, we'll..." She trailed off uncertainly there, one ear twitching, and looked up at the sky. The rest of the night's stars stayed stubbornly put.

Prish shook out a blanket from the back of the cart. "Camping it is," she said, with all the enthusiasm she could scrape together (not much, but more would have been unconvincing anyway). She folded the blanket in half and spread it on the ground, where she and Alsing could curl up side by side and share warmth. She glanced over her shoulder at Otra, who turned three tight circles like a hound before collapsing to the ground in a boneless heap. There were sure to be grass stains on blouse and trousers alike before this was over, but at least Otra seemed content enough where she was. Content enough not to ask Prish and Alsing to budge up, certainly. Perhaps rocks didn't mind the cold overmuch, and thank the skies for that.

"Good night," said Alsing, when they were warmly ensconced under the rest of the blankets and Prish's head was wedged firmly against the soft curve of her neck. "Hopefully we can get some sleep like this."

Prish laughed, ruffling Alsing's fur. "I expect we'll be moving stiffly tomorrow." A soft groan of preemptive discomfort escaped Alsing. "But that's about the worst that can happen to us out here."

"Oh, don't say that," said Otra from across the clearing. "I mean, I'm a stone, so I can't imagine anything particularly dire can happen to *me*. But you're practically inviting disaster, don't you think?"

Prish thought to herself that she could hardly invite disaster when disaster had already arrived and put on a pair of her shoes. But when she opened her mouth, only a mighty yawn issued forth, and before she knew it, she was sound asleep.

———◆———

Before it was light out, Prish awoke to the frantic clatter of attempted petty larceny.

She was up on her feet before she was fully awake: a dangerous combination. "Stop!" she shouted. "Get your stony bottom off that bike right this second or I'll—"

But the person on the bike wasn't Otra at all. A human boy stared back at her from his precarious position atop the bike seat. By her best estimation, his age fell somewhere in the muddy middle ground between child and teenager. "Sorry," he said, recovering his wits enough to apologize for the theft currently underway, "But I need it more than you do." And he put his head down to ride off.

He didn't get far. He had had the presence of mind to unhitch the bike from the cart, but not, apparently, to test the height of the bicycle seat before attempting to ride it away. The toes of one shoe only just grazed the ground when he pushed off, and he teetered twice before he and the bike fell over sideways and landed in a heap.

"Oh, for heaven's sake," said Alsing, who had awoken during the ruckus. She shed the pile of blankets as she hurried over to the boy, leaving a trail of puddled flannel and printed cotton behind her. "Are you all right, little one?"

"A thief in the night!" cried Otra excitedly, darting around the periphery of the action. When she clapped her hands, it sounded like a hammer striking brick, and even she winced at the sound she'd made. "Well. A thief in the dawn." As Alsing extracted the boy from the bicycle, she darted in and snatched the overstuffed pack off his back. "That means we get to thieve you right back, it's only fair."

"Give that back!" The boy lunged for Otra.

A slender but strong hand on his sleeve held him back. "Don't you go running off on me, now," Alsing clucked. She lifted his arms and turned his head this way and that, checking him all over for scrapes and scratches. "You could have gotten yourself well and hurt, taking a fall like that!"

Of course Alsing would go coddling the boy. Prish sighed heavily as she righted the bicycle and gave it, too, a quick once-over for damage. No harm done, that she could see. "What were you thinking," she said, rounding on the boy, "stealing the only means of transport from a pair of old women alone in the woods?"

"Not *that* old, surely," muttered Alsing.

"Nor *that* alone," sang out Otra. In the past moments she had managed to unearth a set of chalk pastels from the boy's pack—leaving most of his other belongings littered on the ground at her feet—and had contrived to draw herself a childish approximation of a face. Two purple eyes, one a bit larger than the other, with stylized lashes and brows; the suggestion of a button nose in black; a curve of pink sketched out a wry smile. "Ta-da! How do I look?"

"Those are mine!" said the boy. A new sheen in his eyes suggested the imminent arrival of tears; Prish took a large step back away from him. She had little enough experience of human children, let alone crying ones. Alsing, apparently content with her examination, let go of him, and he ran over to grab the pastel box out of Otra's open hands. "Look," he said, turning and holding them out, as if he expected Prish or Alsing to litigate the matter. "She ruined them. She—"

He paused and took another look at Otra. Then he scrambled away, putting Alsing between him and her. "What *is* that?"

"*That* is a *her*," said Otra. "*She* is a *who*." She punctuated this with a rude noise as she bent down and continued ruffling through the boy's things. Prish found herself pinched between the desire to annoy the would-be thief and the sense that nothing good would come of giving Otra free reign. "Stop that," she said half-heartedly. "And, to be fair, most of the *who's* I know have faces."

Unsurprisingly, Otra did *not* stop that. "Quite right! And that's why *I* should get the pastels, rather than someone who already has the privilege of a face. I've plainly made a better use of them than he could have."

"Starstruck always think they're so much better than everyone else!" Although he embarked on this statement with rage, it bled away as he spoke, leaving him with only embarrassment. "Just—just because you put your grubby hands on them doesn't make them yours."

Prish scoffed. "Well! Look who learned his talking points from the worst cretins in the schoolyard. Fine thoughts on entitlement from a would-be bicycle thief."

"Enough, *all* of you." The briefest of targeted frowns told Prish that what Alsing actually meant was *especially you, dear heart*. "Otra, put his things down. Pack them up the way you found them." Incredibly, Otra obeyed, albeit not before she heaved a tragic, put-upon sigh.

Alsing's full attention had returned to the human boy; she set her hands on his shoulders before he could consider taking off again. He had shaggy dark brown hair, almost the same friendly color as old coffee grounds ready for the compost heap; his eyes and skin were more nondescript shades of medium and light brown, respectively. He and Alsing were more or less of a height, which meant he would be receiving the full intensity of those soft golden eyes. Prish had been in the same position more than once (or, to be exact, a few inches above it). A look like that and you could find yourself inventing crimes to admit and apologize for, just for a moment to warm yourself by that light of understanding and forgiveness.

"Now tell me," Alsing insisted, firmly and gently and absolutely irrevocably. "What under all the good and giving skies is this all about?"

The boy's name was Wick, he told them over a piece of stale bread with jam, and he was on his way to the Midland Lows, where his aunt and her wife lived, as well as a handful of cousins from his father's side of the family. One of them would surely have a place for him, he asserted, staring at the crumbs that had fallen between his crossed ankles. Now that he was all alone in the world. He was sorry about the bicycle, he told Prish's knees. It had seemed a faster way to get to where he wanted to be, to get to the people who would want him to be there with them. She had the sense that his regret was real, but also that he would have found a way to live with it easily enough if he'd managed to make off with the bicycle.

"But how did you come to be alone?" Alsing pressed. If it had been left up to her, Prish would have just as soon left it alone, but Alsing had a sense for these things: when to let matters lie and when to puncture a hole that would relieve the building pressure. "What happened to your parents?"

He and his mother and father, he told them, had all lived out in the woods, not far from here. He'd left the evening before and walked all through the night. "They abandoned me," he said tightly, and threw the tough breadcrust away from him into the bushes.

In spite of herself, Prish felt a twinge of pity. She hadn't had parents of her own, of course, but she'd sort of helped raise scores of new starstruck, albeit very briefly in each case. To her it seemed nonsensical to go to the extensive trouble of managing a child for—what, ten years? Twelve? Fourteen? She really was awful with human ages—and then walk away from him just when he was tall enough to dust on top of the cupboards and reach the plates down from the higher shelves. "Maybe they just got delayed," she offered. "Or they had an accident, or something. Are they farmers? Woodcutters?" She stumbled over the last offering in her list, glancing at Alsing as she did. "Trappers?"

"They left a note," said Wick shortly.

And this was exactly why Prish usually left the push-or-let-it-be decisions to Alsing, who cast an aggrieved glance at her now over the boy's head. "...Sorry," she said. "Wick. Honestly. I'm sorry."

"My goodness." Otra fanned herself with a leafy branch she'd found on the ground. "A little tact never goes amiss, you know."

"Otra," said Alsing briskly, "you're in charge of finishing breakfast. You're to help Wick find what he needs in the cart if he's still hungry when he's finished there. Prish, can I talk to you privately for a moment?"

"I'm in charge!" Otra clapped her hands with a loud crack that made both Wick and Prish wince. "I've never been in charge of anything before. This is wonderfully exciting!"

"How can you be in charge of breakfast when you don't even eat?" objected Wick, whereupon Otra stuck one finger in the jam pot and smashed it against the general region of her face where she'd drawn herself a mouth.

Prish hurried ahead of Alsing to an out-of-earshot distance before she had to listen to the fallout from that. "Look," she said, for Alsing's ears only, "I told the kid I was sorry, and I meant it. He's old enough to accept a sincere apology." Probably. She doubted Alsing had a much more specific sense of his age, anyway.

"What?" Alsing shook her head. "Oh, no, you did fine! It's not that at all, dear heart." She inspected the front of Prish's sweater and picked loose a crumb of bread. "...We should go with him."

"Go with him," echoed Prish, without comprehension. Her thoughts churned directionlessly, flitting over who *he* might be and what sort of places might be involved in *going*.

"Prish. He's just a boy! It's a long way to the Midland Lows—"

"A *very* long way." Prish looked over Alsing's shoulder at the boy. He sat hunched over another piece of bread while Otra rooted enthusiastically in the baskets on the cart. She held up a can of tinned fish, and Wick shook his head vigorously. "You have customers expecting us..."

"I'll give them a discount for the inconvenience," said Alsing. "I'm sure it will be terrible for Mrs. Willowbotham to go without her new set of embroidered handkerchiefs for an extra week, but she'll have to be very brave about it."

"More like *I'll* have to be very brave pulling a cart with all your damn mending in it," Prish said, shoring up her soured mood with an effort at humor. The road to Eltomel had grown longer than ever, miles and miles and miles between her and Alsing and a quiet out-of-the-way apartment and a rooftop garden. But it seemed the decision had been made. She mustered a smile anyway, and kissed Alsing on the flat spot atop her head, where a tuft of soft red-brown fur stuck up awry from a night spent on the ground. "Of course, Whiskers. If that's what you want to do. It's not *so* far out of the way."

An indignant squawk called their attention back to the other two, who had given up on breakfast preparations in favor of wrestling back and forth on the ground. Otra had a clear weight advantage, and had Wick pinned before Alsing and Prish could pull them apart.

"Make her give them back!" Wick shouted, straining against Prish's arms. (Prish also had a weight advantage against him, though certainly less of one than an embodied paperweight.) "They're not hers!"

"They're not yours, either," said Otra primly. She did not require further restraint from Alsing; in fact, she had disengaged altogether to study the kid leather gloves in which her hands were newly encased. "Your fingers are altogether too thick. You'd never get them even halfway on."

Wick made one more valiant effort at escape before sagging against Prish's arms. She almost dropped him with the sudden change of momentum. "They're *my* mother's," he said desperately, looking to Prish for help or validation.

Otra answered first. "Then why on earth would you want them?" She adjusted the button at one wrist. "Sweet skies above! What a dreadful thing to keep a souvenir of."

"Otra," said Alsing. She kept her voice quiet but infused it with tremendous disappointment. "Be kind."

Otra's shoulders instantly sagged. "But I need them," she wheedled, curving her body inward as she held her hands against herself. "Please?"

Prish was already done with the conversation. "They're not hers to give, and they're not yours to take." She set Wick firmly and fully back on his own two feet. "Give them back and let's all get on with our day." The Midland Lows were far enough, but the distance would feel a lot farther if they went squabbling all the way.

"I hope you appreciate," she told Wick, as she reattached the bicycle to the cart, "that we're going out of our way on your behalf."

The boy shrugged indifferently. She wasn't sure if this was typical teenage (pre-teen?) affect or if he was still annoyed at her for suggesting that his parents had just wandered off for a bit. "I didn't ask you to."

"Hm." She let the hitch fall slack and pushed the bicycle a few feet, making sure it was soundly attached. "The thing about stealing a person's only mode of transportation is that you might sort of read it as an invitation to tag along to make sure there aren't any further cases of highway robbery." Her little toolbox had stayed behind on the ground by his feet; she nodded at it. "Bring that here and I'll lower the seat a bit for you."

He picked up the toolbox, but hesitated, looking between Prish and the bicycle.

"Come on, then." A hurry-up gesture did nothing to stir him. "I don't bite. Alsing's the one with proper teeth."

While she snorted at her own joke, Wick shuffled a half step farther away. "I've never ridden a bicycle before," he confessed in a tumble.

She chose not to mention the extra layer of poor sense involved, in that case, in his attempt to make off with one undetected. "Everyone who's ever ridden one had to learn sometime," she said, and moved closer to grab the toolbox from him. "Might as well be today."

With the seat at its lowest, the bicycle was more or less suited to Wick's height. Their first progress that morning was slow, as he teetered along at somewhat less than a snail's pace; Alsing and Otra walked on ahead after an incident wherein Otra professed a deep concern that her important destiny might center somehow on bicycles and the ability to ride one. Or, perhaps, she supposed, a bicycle might lead her to that destiny.

"I don't see how it's fair," Prish heard her ranting, despite the distance between them. She couldn't make out Alsing's hushed response, but Otra's follow-up refused to go unheard. "Well, I never even had parents in the first place! Surely that's *much* more tragic."

When she glanced at Wick, his forehead had developed a deep crease down the middle; a crease that she doubted was bicycle derived, as he'd begun to get the rhythm of the thing. He surprised her, though, when he said: "I'm confused. We're going back the same way I came."

"Well, if that's the case, it's even more important that you have a capable couple of babysitters along for the trip." With a vague gesture she indicated the path ahead. "If you kept going south, you would hit the Wendlyway Gorge. You'd have done all right if you were a bird, I reckon, but: you're not. We have to go up and around before turning south again."

"Oh," said Wick quietly, and that was all.

For a good long while, there was nothing but the regular sound of the tires over the bumpy ground and Wick's rapid breath. It was nice to walk in the quiet, under the shade afforded them by the close-grown trees to either side of the path. It was also nice to have someone with young legs who could take a turn pedaling. It would have been nicer still, she thought, to be walking in the quiet and the shade with her wife by her side. "You ought to stop," she said finally. "Don't want you to be sore tomorrow."

"It hasn't been that long," he complained, but when he got down, he was already moving stiffly.

Once she took his place, he kept pace alongside her instead of joining the others. Not that she blamed him for avoiding Otra's company, but she'd sort of expected that he might just as soon avoid *hers*, too. Conversation was Alsing's strong suit—Prish had never even developed the habit of talking to the plants in her garden—and she composed and discarded any number of opening forays into the fine art before surrendering to a trip in pleasant, if crisp, silence.

They stopped at midday for a meal and to rest their weary legs; Prish had kept a careful eye all morning on Alsing's limp, which seemed no better nor any worse. Before she could be instructed otherwise, Otra nominated herself for the responsibility of handing out lunch, seconded the motion, and provided the affirmative vote to secure herself the position. This meant that lunch consisted of pickled beets and candied peaches laid out side by soggy side atop a wedge of bread. ("The colors just go together so beautifully!") At least the mingled vinegar and treacle took the edge off the increasingly stale crust.

Before they set off again, Alsing took Prish by the elbow, bringing her mouth close to Prish's ear. "I think there's some rain coming on," she said quietly, and though Prish couldn't see much of the blue sky through the branches, she knew without a doubt they'd be in for a soaking. Alsing always felt such things in her bones, and seeing as Prish had none of those, she deferred to her wife's judgment. "If you spot anyplace that could serve as a likely shelter—"

"I'll keep an eye out," Prish promised. Getting drenched meant walking in wet shoes, which meant blisters at best and root-rot at worst, and it was no use either letting the cold get its hooks into Alsing. "Don't you worry." Worrying was *Prish's* job, after all. "We'll be fine."

Wick made a small noise from behind them. "I know where we can go," he told the pebbles under their shoes.

———◆———

The house to which Wick led them had been built into the side of a hill. The roof overhung the building far enough for them to roll the bike and cart underneath, although it required them to climb over the hitch to get inside, which they did slightly before the heavens parted and the rains poured out.

The house looked small from the outside, and even smaller once they had all piled inside. Partly this had to do with the absolute scale of the place: a single room downstairs and a narrow ladder that led, Wick said, to two even tinier bedrooms above. And partly it was because of the absolute magnitude of clutter overlaying every surface, flat or otherwise. Some things were obviously the trappings of a young person—the Wick-sized jacket flung onto the kitchen counter, the math textbook splayed open over one arm of a wooden chair. Prish picked up a jar full of colorless marbles and gave it a testing shake. Pretty sad marbles, she thought, all clear glass and all the same size. The poor kid must not have had any other children to play with. Depressing.

Some other things must have belonged to his absent parents. Prish poked one finger into a leather-bound journal bookmarked with an ink pen and squinted briefly at the cobwebby handwriting clinging to every page. Something about *thaumaturgical flux*, *base rate of emission*; the word *magic* jumped out at Prish from the middle of another scribbled paragraph. Magic? Sweet and sacred skies. The boy's parents must have been the kind of crackpots who believed some other, free-floating source of magic divorced from what moved a starstruck soul was out there waiting to be discovered. Obviously they hadn't been prize-winning parents on any account, but this added a whole new flavor of oddball. Otra pulled the pen out of the journal and began drawing swirls of vines down the back of her opposite hand and arm.

Other items defied obvious categorization: fine tools, bits of unfinished or torn-up mechanisms whose purpose Prish couldn't begin to guess. The wires were as delicate as root hairs, the gears no bigger than pumpkin seeds. They'd left a telescope angled so that its lens peered upward, through the front window. That would've been a helpful sort of thing for Prish and Alsing to have, back in their previous life, though Prish thought twice before making such a remark out loud.

"I thought you said your parents were—" Prish began instead, but trailed off. Farmers, woodcutters, trappers, she'd said, but Wick had never actually answered one way or another.

"Natural philosophers?" said Alsing tentatively.

The boy shrugged, fiddling with the handle of a kitchen drawer. "You can sleep in their room tonight, if you want."

"What about me?" Otra pressed. She'd picked up the journal that Prish had peeked into, and was paging eagerly through it. "Where can I sleep? Or: where *would* I sleep, if I were the sort of person who slept?"

"No one's sleeping yet," Alsing said, poking a hole in Wick's agitation before it could inflate to its full proportions. "Wick, would it be all right if I look through the cupboards? I see there's wood for the stove—I'll make us a hot supper."

"Help yourself," said Wick, and slung himself into the chair in the corner, dislodging the math textbook. "It's not as if my mom and dad are here to say no." He stared out the window, watching the wind fling fat droplets against the wavy glass.

The cupboards were well stocked, and Alsing gave Otra the task of boxing up whatever she could find that would travel well and fit on the cart. It gave Otra something harmless to do other than be in Alsing's way as she puttered around the stove, and Prish was relieved Alsing had thought of it. Another kitchen chair had been shoved to one side and covered in a deep sediment of discarded belongings; Prish took a moment to excavate it from under five sweaters and jackets, several stacked and creased papers, a leather case the size and approximate shape of a tea kettle, and an unwashed dinner plate. It felt good to sit in the emptied chair and rest her weary legs—just for a moment, she thought, and then she could help Alsing prepare the meal.

The next thing she knew, the front window had gone dark, and the house had developed a pleasant tomato-y smell. Wick had been evicted from his own chair, apparently under Alsing's request. He sang softly under his breath as he set out (clean, Prish hoped) tableware on the unearthed kitchen table. "*The mountain is my pillow,*" he sang. "*The green earth is my cloak.*"

Alsing plunked a bowl of boiled potatoes into the middle of the table and beamed at him. "Pretty song, isn't it?"

A handful of spoons clattered to the floor. "You know it?" Wick said urgently.

"Hmm? Oh, no." Alsing started to stoop to collect the fallen cutlery, but he ducked down faster and scooped them up before she could. "I just liked the sound of it. What is it called?"

"I don't..." Wick put his back to her and set the spoons out, one at a time, a sharp click as each one struck the tabletop. "It's something my mom used to sing to me. I think."

A stab of pity caught Prish in the gut, folding her over. She and Alsing exchanged a worried look behind the boy's back. "Well," Alsing said, with careful lightness, as Prish straightened gingerly up. "It's fine enough. How does the rest of it go?"

"I don't know," he said thickly, and installed himself in one of the kitchen chairs, hunched over his folded arms.

Alsing did not, of course, scold him for having his elbows on the table. While she put the finishing touches on the meal, Prish did her best impression of someone who had *not* just woken up. She stretched and bent over to straighten up the pile of papers she'd set aside earlier, which she must have disturbed during her unintended nap.

One of them, though, caught her eye with the two words printed carefully at the top: *Dear Wick*.

She glanced at the person in question, who maintained his profound slouch at the table, and twitched the paper farther out of the pile to read on. The handwriting was different than the fine spidery writing in the journal she'd seen earlier, simple and stark, but there was a forced quality to it, as if the writer had pressed too hard with the pen.

> *Dear Wick,*
>
> *I don't know when you'll be back—soon, I hope. Your father and I couldn't wait, not a moment more, not once we held them. Yours will be along soon and then you'll understand, too. We love you and nothing will change when we're more than we were before, and it won't be long before you—*

The paper twitched out of Prish's grasp, and Otra loomed over her, wagging a finger. "It's rude to snoop," she said.

"I beg your—"

"Time to eat!" said Alsing brightly, clearly trying to forestall additional friction.

Prish gave Otra a dark look but levered herself to her feet and shuffled toward the table. "Time to eat," she echoed pointedly, as Otra studied the paper.

Otra responded by tapping the smeared line of pink chalk across the bottom of her face, and settled into the seat Prish had just vacated. There was nothing else for Prish to do but give up and join the others for supper, even though the lack of a fourth chair meant she had to stand beside the table cradling a bowl against her chest. It was, unsurprisingly, a quiet meal; Otra stayed uncharacteristically silent even after she'd finished reading the note, and no one else had much to say beyond a murmured thanks to Alsing for the lovely tomato soup and the bean-and-onion confit she had magicked up from the cans in the cupboard and the remnants in the root cellar.

A unanimous decision was reached for an early bedtime (though Otra insisted on fetching a bucket of water to wash the dinner dishes first). The double bed creaked under Prish's weight when she flopped atop it with a sigh. Alsing paused beside the bed to part the curtains, sending down a shower of dust. Either Wick hadn't been entirely forthright about how long he'd been on his own, or (perhaps the more obvious answer, considering the state of the downstairs) his parents hadn't been particularly tidy people. With a *tsk-tsk*, Alsing took a clean shirt off a laundry pile in the corner and used it to swipe up a long gray smudge of the lingering dust from the sill and the top of the curtain rod. "She's still out there," she noted, and swung the window open. Her ears twitched as she leaned her cheek against the glass. "Do you think she's having trouble finding the well?"

Prish sat up. Outside, a flash of color and movement indicated Otra's presence between two of the trees. "Wick told her the well was within sight of the house. She can't get *that* lost." As soon as she said it, she heard how foolish she sounded. Otra could probably get lost without ever leaving the kitchen. "...I'll go out and look for her in a few minutes. If we don't hear her come back in."

"Oh," said Alsing, "oh, look..."

Prish followed the angle of her outstretched arm and found the single star streaking across the sky. Even as she came up onto her knees for a better view, the light vanished into the treetops. Both she and Alsing held their breath, waiting.

They stared out longer than they needed to, longer than they should have had to wait. There was no flash of light, no thunderclap to tell the tale of a vole or oak or earthworm trying to get ahold of the double-edged sword of consciousness for the first time. A star, yes; but no starstruck.

Neither moved. Still watching, still waiting. Still wondering. Prish should say something, she felt, should break the brittle silence. Alsing deserved reassurance, or better yet, true hope. But Prish didn't know how to offer what she didn't already have in hand. She gave up the vigil first, letting herself drop back down onto the bed. Alsing crawled in more carefully alongside her. Age and use had worn a deep indentation in the middle of the mattress, one that nudged them together at the halfway point, and they nestled together, arms and legs wound loosely together. Neither spoke—what was there to say?—and after a few minutes, they heard the front door unlatch and Otra enter, humming tunelessly.

A splash, a faint clatter of dishware, and the noise from below faded quickly to the background of Prish's awareness as Alsing began to play with one of the long green fronds that made up Prish's hair. "He'll be all right, I think," she said. "The boy." She kept her voice low, mindful of the thin wall between them and the *he* in question. "It'll take time. And care. We'll see what these relatives in the Midland Lows are like."

"We'll see, will we? And what will we do if you decide they're not up to snuff?" Prish tweaked Alsing's nose. "Keep him like that horrible stray cat we had our first year in the city?"

"You liked that cat."

"No." Prish closed her eyes, and not only because sleep was calling her name. She was tired in body and in spirit and in whatever glue held the two together. "Not really. But I liked *you*."

They lay folded together in silence for a moment. Maybe if they'd left a little space between them, there would have been room for the things she didn't want to say. Alsing made the first brave venture into the lull, with hopeful teasing in her voice: "You just had a grudge because it bit you that once."

"Hmm," said Prish, and chose to meet her where the invitation led. "I'll bite you once, too, and we'll see how you like it."

"I reckon I'll like it just fine."

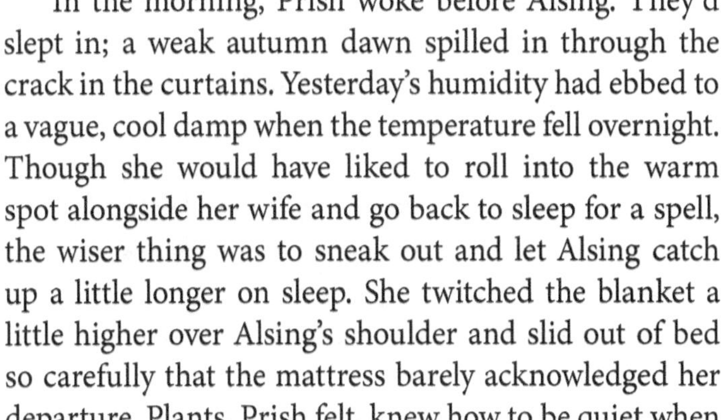

In the morning, Prish woke before Alsing. They'd slept in; a weak autumn dawn spilled in through the crack in the curtains. Yesterday's humidity had ebbed to a vague, cool damp when the temperature fell overnight. Though she would have liked to roll into the warm spot alongside her wife and go back to sleep for a spell, the wiser thing was to sneak out and let Alsing catch up a little longer on sleep. She twitched the blanket a little higher over Alsing's shoulder and slid out of bed so carefully that the mattress barely acknowledged her departure. Plants, Prish felt, knew how to be quiet when they needed to.

The door to Wick's cupboard-sized room stood open. Once Prish had tiptoed down the stairs, she opened the front door and peered over the bicycle to find him out on the porch, perched on the little stool that stood there. Otra was nowhere to be seen, but Prish could hear her voice in snatches somewhere nearby. After a moment, she appeared briefly amid a copse of trees, whereupon she waved vigorously at Prish and Wick, then disappeared into the misty wood again.

"She's checking the trees for nests," Wick said. "Apparently." He didn't look over at Prish, but his tone begged her to agree with what he'd left unsaid.

"Sacred skies!" said Prish, obliging him. "It's autumn. If there were nests with babies in them, they would've frozen last night."

He managed half a smile, though whatever reserves he pulled good humor from must have been running deeply in the red by now. "When are we leaving?"

"Soon." Instead of making Alsing's excuses for her, Prish clambered over the bicycle hitch and found a stick in the yard. The damp mud from last night's rain made a suitable canvas for her to sketch out a rough map in front of where Wick sat. "Today we'll reach the Duke's Highway. We should make it to Wandleham—" She tapped the cluster of crude houses she'd drawn. "—by tomorrow midday or so, if the going is good. From there, it's only another two or three days to the Lows."

Wick studied the sketch. "I didn't know we had dukes. Or that they had highways."

Prish tapped the stick against the side of her leg. "Of course we don't have dukes anymore," she said, with more confidence than she felt. Really she should know more about this than a child. *Alsing* would have known. "If you're going to be a duke, you might as well build highways as anything else. Because of, you know. Trade." She tossed the stick aside into the overgrown grass by the porch. "Commerce. And all of that."

"Okay," said Wick, unconvinced.

Alsing rose half an hour later. She was annoyed at having been permitted to oversleep so long, but not so annoyed that she couldn't explain, at length, as they ate a bit of breakfast, that the individual in question had been one Duke Jaquintine VII, who had widened the pre-existing paths in order to improve trade routes between the major cities, that all of this had happened roughly three hundred years ago, and that there hadn't been any dukes since the era of Jaquintine's grandson, Duke Anwintine IX, who had been overthrown by his people and who had been eaten by a starstruck wolf before he could be fully driven from his castle.

"Have you ever eaten anybody?" Wick asked, though he sounded much more intrigued about the prospect than worried.

Alsing gave him a teasing shove of the shoulder. "Not *yet*."

"What if you ate someone who was going to be starstruck, though?" mused Otra. The table only had three chairs to sit in, so she wandered about while pushing dry oats around the bottom of a bowl with a spoon. She cocked her head as the other three stared at her, aghast. "I don't mean on purpose, obviously. But before they were, or you were?" She tapped her spoon against her chin with an audible click. "Not that it matters to me. I seem to be thoroughly inedible in any case."

"Otra," said Prish. "Those are Wick's gloves you're wearing again."

"No they're not," said Otra automatically, even as she dropped the bowl and plopped onto the sofa with her hands beneath her.

"Give them *back*." Prish stood up so fast the bowls clattered on the table. "I've had just about enough of this, Otra. Some things just aren't for you and I'm not sure why you don't understand that."

Otra wriggled but kept her hands where they were. "They feel nice," she whined. "No one else is wearing them! Why shouldn't I put them to proper use?"

"Give them to me." Prish stuck one hand in front of Otra's chalked-on face. "Why don't you sit for a minute with the idea that maybe your destiny ought to involve taking up a little less *space* around here?"

"Prish." Alsing's ears lay low behind her head. "We're all tired. Don't take it out on Otra. And Otra: Wick's reasons for wanting to keep the gloves are no concern of yours. Give them back, please."

Otra deflated but didn't argue as she stripped the gloves off and tossed them on the floor by Wick's feet. She left the bowl of oats atop a pile of old magazines and went to go sit outside, alone.

"It's just gloves," muttered Prish, "for goodness' sake," and wasn't sure who she was talking to.

Before setting the bicycle's tires back on the path, Prish gave Otra's additions to the cart a brief once-over. She hadn't overdone it, to Prish's best judgment; the cart would still be towable. Prish was surprised to see the leather case wedged in between a pair of apple boxes. "What's this doing here?" she demanded.

"Oh," Otra said. "Oh!" She leaned over the side of the cart and tucked the leather case into a more secure position. She had already, it seemed, forgotten the morning's brief segue into glove-related discourse. "I thought to myself, wouldn't that be just the perfect thing to carry jars in to make sure they don't crack together and break wide open?" She tilted her head to the side. "Or eggs. Or jars of eggs! Say, do I get to try the bicycle today?"

"No," Prish said, and amended, with a sideways glance at Alsing: "Maybe tomorrow. The tool kit is at the bottom of the cart now anyway."

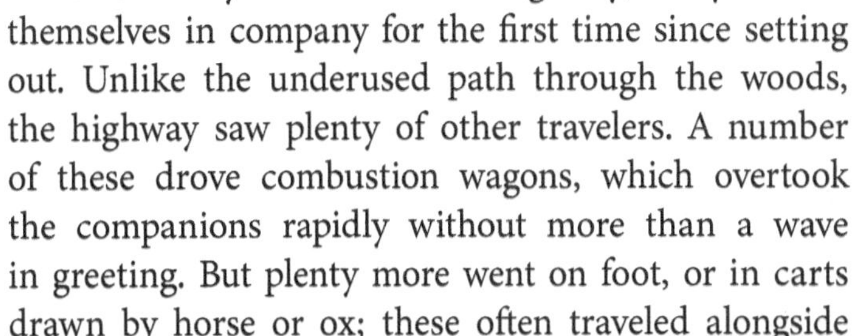

Once they reached the highway, they found themselves in company for the first time since setting out. Unlike the underused path through the woods, the highway saw plenty of other travelers. A number of these drove combustion wagons, which overtook the companions rapidly without more than a wave in greeting. But plenty more went on foot, or in carts drawn by horse or ox; these often traveled alongside Prish's party for an hour or two, until a difference in pace or a demand for rest could no longer be ignored by one side or the other.

Now that they were on the highway, Prish didn't mind taking more than her due share of bicycle time. It was far easier to pedal on the packed-dirt road than on the rocky, rain-ribbed path through the woods, and besides, she was content to let Alsing socialize. It was Alsing, after all, who could swap potage recipes and pickling tips, who didn't mind coaxing a toddler out of a tantrum or trading a jar of jam for fresh butter. Prish, on the other hand, had always been better at plants than at people.

With one notable exception, perhaps. Her heart threatened to tear itself loose from its nook inside her when she watched Alsing reluctantly hand a starstruck bear cub back to his adopted mother, a lumpy, genial starstruck potato. If Alsing sensed Prish looking, she didn't show it. She kept pace beside the young mother, talking loudly, gesturing expressively. Her words didn't make it all the way back to Prish, but their too-bright, too-brittle tone did.

While Prish pedaled, Wick hung back beside her, even when their fellow travelers included humans or starstruck around his own age. He plodded along in silence, breaking it only with the occasional aggrieved sigh when Otra tore past amid a horde of laughing, shrieking children. She tried exactly once to tag him into a game of chase, an invitation he received with distaste. "Don't touch me," he snapped. "What's the matter with you?" And after that she contented herself exclusively with other company.

Children seemed to delight in Otra's attention, skipping alongside her, singing the silly nonsense songs that she made up for them on the fly. She answered their questions about her nature gamely, whether they were addressed to her with genuine interest, or, in a few cases, what sounded more like morbid curiosity: "Yes, I'm brand new! Just two days old. Or maybe some several thousand, depending on how you do your accounting." "Rock all the way through. You can give me a knock on the back if you like, to test it out, but I don't expect your knuckles will thank you for it." "Well, of course I could still see if you wiped the eyes off my face! What a rude thing to say."

When there were no children around, and if Alsing was otherwise occupied, Otra walked by herself, sometimes picking the desiccated wildflowers that lined the road, sometimes carrying a particularly long branch or that leather case she'd stowed in the cart. Once, as she trudged along staring (presumably) off into space, Prish nearly felt moved to an attempt at bridge-building: asking her what she was thinking about, perhaps.

Before she could say a word, though, Otra swiveled toward her. "I think I'm getting very close to working out what my destiny is," she announced, which instantly smothered the already damp kindling of Prish's interest. "Do you want to hear about it?"

"Maybe later," Prish said hastily, and pedaled a little faster.

Over the course of the day, one of the few travelers who chose to keep pace with Prish and Wick was a middle-aged starstruck horse, who rode a sway-backed mare. "A little awkward, isn't it?" said the starstruck by way of greeting, patting her mount's neck. "Sort of like if you were to eat a turnip, I suppose."

"She's a radish, actually," said Wick, and looked at Prish as if to verify this.

"And I eat radishes often enough," Prish said, with a shrug. "Turnips, too."

The other starstruck, who gave her name as Tilla, found this very funny. As they rode, she pointed out the rest of her family: her husband—a human man—his sister and brother-in-law, a sizable passel of nieces and nephews.

"You're married to a human?" Wick asked, and Prish was so startled by the rudeness that she lost hold of her effort to remember one or two of the names she'd been given. To cover her embarrassment, she hurried, in turn, to indicate the rest of her own party. She indicated Alsing, whom she noted as her wife. "And this is—Wick," she said, lacking a suitable noun phrase to describe him in kind. He waved a hand in greeting. "And that one over there is Otra."

"A fine group," said Tilla, who gave no indication that she'd noticed Prish's incomplete introductions. "You looking for work in Wrightscross or Wandleham? We've heard there's good jobs to be had. Well. We've heard there's *jobs* to be had, anyway."

"I suppose we will be looking for work. We'll head back to Eltomel first, though. Me and Alsing. Don't know what we'll end up doing. We'd been living in the Craftwood...it had a good view of the skies." Prish adjusted her grip on the handlebars; her shoulders had begun to ache with the strain. "Alsing liked to meet the new ones."

"Oh," said Tilla, sadly and sympathetically.

"The new what?" Wick asked, his face crinkling with confusion. "What about the sky?"

Prish and Tilla exchanged a glance over his head. He'd moved out into the Craftwood a year or two ago, he'd said; that hadn't left him many sources to hear about the disappearance of starstruck. "Didn't your parents ever mention the, uh—" Prish gestured vaguely overhead. "That there weren't any more stars falling? No more starstruck?"

"I like to think they're still landing," said Tilla wistfully. "Somewhere in the antipodes. A whole upside-down land full of starstruck."

"They didn't really talk to me about—stuff like that." Wick picked up a stick and began idly whacking at the roadside weeds that passed. "Do *you* wish you lived on the other side of the world?"

"Well, hardly!" Tilla laughed. "The most long-distance I can handle in a relationship is when Jostam gets up before me to make breakfast."

That wasn't what quite what Wick had been asking, Prish thought, but she didn't press it. They rode on for a while without speaking: the creak of the cart wheels and the *clip-clop* of the old mare's hooves making idle conversation of their own. Finally, Prish ventured: "Is anyone...doing anything about it?"

"Is there anything to be done?" Tilla shrugged and tossed her forelock. "Jostam and his family make the right *too-bad-very-sad* noises. But we can't very well keep going past Wrightscross all the way to the stars to check into the situation, can we?" The reins twitched in her hands, left and right and left again. Prish wondered how old she'd been when the star had found her; if she'd had a chance to resign herself to the taste of a bit in her mouth and the tug of someone else's will. "Maybe it's my fault, too, if all of us just...stop."

"Maybe it's not anyone's fault," Prish said, attempting reassurance without a lot of practical experience to draw on. "Maybe it just *is*."

"Lots of things just *are*." Tilla tossed her head so that her gray-streaked mane flapped in the wind. Up ahead, Otra flitted across the highway, a strange vision in orange and purple that made Tilla's mare hedge for a moment. "But a woman can't help but wonder what else they could be."

When they parted ways with another group, Prish put extra effort into pushing the pedals, so that she caught up with Alsing. "You're limping," she said, in between heavy breaths. "Worse than before. We should stop to rest again."

Alsing made a dismissive gesture with one paw. "I'll let you know if I need to stop," she said, in a tight tone that told Prish for certain that they should have stopped an hour ago. "Don't mother me."

"You insist on mothering the *entire rest of the world*, my darling, so forgive me if I think fair's fair."

Alsing stopped walking, and Prish coasted to a halt beside her. She hadn't liked the feel of those words in her own mouth, the way she'd broken away the tender edges of those words—*my darling*—left only the sharp bones beneath. "Sorry," she amended belatedly, and didn't try to embroider the threadbare apology with empty excuses. "Is it better if you ride the cycle, or worse?"

"Worse."

Prish let that hang in the air a little while, unsure how best to bat it away. "If you want to press on..."

"For a little while yet," Alsing said, and moved off again. Prish let her gain some distance first before leaning into the pedals once more. The wheels turned slowly over the dry, sandy road, and the white tip of Alsing's lashing tail never quite vanished into the clouds of dust that blew up behind her footfalls.

By evening, Alsing's limp had worsened enough that even Otra noticed, and she couldn't feign it away anymore. They weren't likely to make it to Wandleham by midday on the morrow, either, Prish thought, or at least not without a new career as horse thieves.

Instead of a life of high crime, they overnighted just off the road, with Alsing curled up reluctantly in the back of the wagon and everyone else on the cool ground. Well—with Wick and Prish on the cool ground. While everyone else settled down to sleep, Otra excused herself to go putter around in the woods again. "It's the sky," she said, before she scuttled off. "It's just like a painting, don't you think?"

It would take an awfully big brush to work on a canvas that size, but Prish was still hard pressed to argue. Above the treetops and ahead of the oncoming dark, the heavens had taken on a hue that was somehow both gold and purple and also not really either of those. It would take an artist to devise a shade like that, she thought, and very likely the assistance of certain hallucinogenic substances.

"It's beautiful," Wick said, his eyes fixed on the sky. "What do you even call a color like that?" Prish could only shrug in answer.

Alsing sat up for a while, keeping an eye on Otra, before Prish convinced her to attempt some sleep. "She won't wander off or she'll lose her captive audience," she said, and withered under Alsing's golden-eyed frown. The heated words they'd exchanged earlier still smoldered between them; Prish attempted to throw some sand over what remained of the argument. "Besides. You can't expect her to just lie there for eight hours. She doesn't sleep. She doesn't eat. She has to do *something*, doesn't she?"

"Poor creature," sighed Alsing, but she lay back down and let Prish draw the faded quilt up over her shoulder.

"Do you have enough blankets for yourself? The ground is so pebbly here..."

"No, it's fine," said Prish, a little more loudly, "I'll sleep on top of Wick if I have to." Wick produced a rude noise in response, and she grinned as she leaned over the edge of the cart to nestle a kiss in the careworn furrow between Alsing's brows.

Before she burrowed down into her own blankets, she heard Wick singing softly to himself: that same funny little song about mountains and pillows and cloaks. Not much of a lullaby, she thought, not without more than a handful of words to go on. But the repetition soothed her enough to slide her over the edge into sleep.

◆

Another night on the ground left everyone in ill temper—except Otra, who only grew more bubbly and good-humored for each unsleeping night she spent. While the others grumbled through a breakfast of old bread and older cheese, she filled their silence with her own empty thoughts: musings on where the stars had gone and why hers was special and what a star would look like, if you could hold it in your hand.

"They look *awfully* small up there," she said, waving vaguely skyward. Her chalked-on face had lost its integrity over the past few days; all that was left was the suggestion of a left eye and a blotchy smear of smile.

"Just a mote of glittery dust, really. They must be bigger up close, though. How big do you suppose?" She held up her hands, framing a watermelon-sized circle. "As big as all that?" One hand closed into a fist. "Or that?" She held up an imaginary shape, no bigger than a cherry, between her thumb and forefinger, and leaned forward across everyone else's half-eaten meal. "Or that? What do *you* think, Wick? Probably you're the most unbiased observer."

"The only thing whose size I care about right now is the knot in my back," said Prish, forestalling the expected retort from Wick. She collected a small scrap of pleasure from his resulting snort. "Someone pass the jam, please?"

Midway through the third morning, small houses and outlying buildings finally started to replace the lonesome woods. By noon, they had entered Wandleham proper: the sprawling outgrowth that had, some hundred years ago, spilled out from the city's old, ivy-grown heart. As they went farther, the white brick buildings rose higher and higher on either side, and rowhouses gave way to apartments, apartments to official-looking buildings and theaters and museums. Most of the traffic moved on foot, on bicycle, or in wagons and carriages, but the occasional combustion engine came roaring through the crowd, while motorists cursed out the aggrieved pedestrians and the pedestrians returned the tirade in kind. Otra stopped in front of the Wandleham Museum of Contemporary Art to point out a poster for an exhibition of paintings. "What if we stopped by just for a moment?" she wheedled.

Prish did not respond well to wheedling. "Absolutely not." They had the coin for a night in an inn, as long as it wasn't too fancy an inn, and not a great deal more than that. "We don't have money to waste on nonsense."

"Prish," murmured Alsing. "I know we don't have the money, but we could afford some patience. She's trying to figure out who she is."

"*What* she is, maybe." Under a cool golden look from Alsing, Wick's scorn curdled to embarrassment, and he fixed his attention on his shoes.

Prish stifled a sigh and turned to Otra. "Sorry for being short with you," she said. "I—sweet skies, I don't know where I'm supposed to look at you. I'm trying, all right?" Some sort of promise felt in order. After a moment's fumbling, Prish came up with: "I'll be...nicer."

"If you like," said Otra obscurely, and brushed past her down the street.

"I'm not sure that's the right way," Prish called after her, whereupon she was forced to confess to the others that she'd never before visited this city, and she hadn't the slightest idea where they might soon find someplace to stay.

"I think I remember," Wick allowed. "We...I used to live here. Before." His cheeks darkened as Prish and Alsing both attempted to look very casual about this new information. "I guess I still know my way around."

They followed him to a great old building slouched around the corner of a main street onto a side alley. The wooden sign above the door depicted a single drooping blossom. There was no telling what color either the flower or the background might have been before the paint faded, some several thousand years ago by the looks of the thing; it could as easily have been yellow as blue or anything in between. It reminded Prish, obscurely, of the indescribable sunset she and Wick had observed.

The raised letters carved at the bottom proclaimed its name to be the Drowsy Marigold. Prish felt a bit of a drowsy marigold herself just then and pronounced it a perfect place to stay. They fastened the bicycle to a nearby post and carried the boxes inside to inquire after vacancy.

The innkeeper, an elderly dandelion with only a few wisps of white fluff still clinging to the back of her head, offered them a clean room and a home-cooked meal whenever they were ready for it. "Now?" asked Wick, with a hopefulness that verged on desperation. With a smile, the innkeeper murmured something nearly inaudible about growing children. An eyeblink later, they'd all been ushered to a table in the dining room, where they sat in weary, brittle silence.

Prish must have nodded off, because the next thing she knew, she had a plate the size of a cart wheel in front of her, piled with grilled tomatoes and onions and thick slabs of buttery-crisp toast and a lovely cut of pork that wallowed invitingly in a pool of fat. With gusto, she set to, pausing only to thank the innkeeper profusely when a cup of black coffee appeared at Alsing's elbow and a saucer of coffee grounds by her own. "Fertilizer," she explained, around a gritty mouthful, as Wick failed to keep himself from gawking.

Once the pace of the meal slowed, the conversation picked up, as did the mood. It was easier to let go of the tension that they'd all pulled tight between them, here in the lap of this little luxury. After they'd all had the chance to fill their bellies (or, in Otra's case, to smear a line of mashed potato across her face), the innkeeper showed them to a quiet corner of the top floor. Before she could even disappear out the door with a whispered *please enjoy your stay*, Alsing had deposited her luggage on the floor and collapsed across the nearest bed. "I'm just going to close my eyes for a moment." The words, delivered facedown into the pillow, mashed together but remained mostly intelligible. "Wake me up after ten minutes."

"Of course, my dear. I promise." Prish whisked the comforter off the other bed and settled it over Alsing, then grabbed Otra by the sleeve and Wick by the shoulder and maneuvered both of them straight back out the door. Both of them were smart enough—or disoriented enough—not to object until she'd gotten them back onto the stairs. "Now look. We're going to let Alsing catch up on her rest, we're going to have a nice afternoon out on the town, and we're either going to get along beautifully—or *tell* her we did."

Prish had lived in Eltomel for two years, before she and Alsing had built their little house in the Craftwood. If she closed her eyes, Wandleham and Eltomel had much in common: the competing smells of fresh bread in the bakeries and stale water in the gutter, the creak of wagon wheels over cobblestones, the background blur of chatter. But when she looked around, it was a different place entirely. Wandleham was bigger, and older, the buildings taller and heaped together in a looming, unfriendly style. Cavernously tall cutaway arches gaped at the top of the city offices and the theater; the facades had been cut from blocks of a sandy-yellow stone, not a red or white brick to be seen. What ornamentation there was around the windows was simple and rather severe, a rectangle of stone of a slightly lighter color; little scrollwork adorned the tops of columns and no brattishing topped off the walls or filled out the tops of those great big arches. Prish decided that while she didn't mind staying a night in the city, she certainly wouldn't like to *live* here.

Wick, having lived in Wandleham before, showed them around with the attention to detail that might be expected of a child whose main experience of the place had been going to school and playing in the squares. Confidently, he waved his arm at an empty cobblestone-paved space and informed them: "This is the market square. People sell stuff here." As they crossed a narrow body of water, he announced, "That's the canal. Or the river? It's probably the canal."

Otra leaned over the railing, peering at the water's surface. Prish sidled closer and took a firm grip on the strap of the little leather case, which Otra had taken to wearing over one shoulder as a kind of purse. "How deep down does it go?" she asked. "Do you think I could learn to swim?"

Prish and Wick very adamantly did *not* think so, but Otra remained unconvinced until she was distracted by the passing of a small cart that had a fat, happy squirrel painted on its side and the smell of roasted nuts trailing after it. They were obliged to follow, and soon found themselves in a small, pleasant green space tucked away in the city's heart. Mature trees cut off much of the noise from the street, and little children played in the mud beside a small pond. A dozen-odd of Wandleham's omnipresent pigeons arrogantly patrolled the space between the food carts that had gathered to serve anyone looking for an afternoon snack. Prish would have called the birds a flock, except that she thought pigeons seemed altogether too self-interested for flocking purposes.

When Wick cast a longing look at a cart selling hand pies, Prish bought him one overstuffed with apples, and, in the name of peace, one for Otra. Wick ate his in three bites, while Otra rubbed hers briefly against her face and then proclaimed that she was quite full. Then Wick ate the rest of that one, too. After that, they found an out-of-the-way spot beneath a fine old linden tree to collapse in the patchwork sunshine that filtered through the canopy. All things considered, Prish might have preferred being in bed beside Alsing to shepherding these two through an unknown city. But, she thought, stretching out so that her face found a patch of light, this wasn't so bad. The price of an extra apple hand pie wasn't so dear, if it came served with a side of getting along.

While she enjoyed the taste of sunlight, Wick took up his travelogue again. "And that's University Tower," he said, highlighting a gleaming bit of glass and metal that could just be made out where the far side of the park ended at a wrought-iron fence. "My mother used to work there. My dad worked at Thullis and Esamyn. They're engineers. Over in the business district." His hand shifted, gesturing vaguely through the trees to the unseen stretch of buildings that lay to the west.

"Oh?" said Otra. She sat cross-legged on the other side of Wick, drawing in the dirt with a stick. "What sort of things did he engineer?"

"...Well," said Wick, with transparently artificial confidence, "you know, machines. And things."

"Naturally." With a flourish, Otra finished her drawing—a sketchy outline of a fox with a familiar smile—and set the stick aside. "And what did your mother do at the university, if I may ask?"

"She was a professor," Wick said with pride. Prish pushed herself up to one elbow, digging a loose root hair out of one eye with the knuckles of her free hand. "She studied the biological-thaumaturgical dichotomy." He pronounced the words carefully, by rote, and conceded before Otra could ask the inevitable follow-up question: "I don't really know what that means."

"*Biological* refers to living things," said Otra. She rested her chin on her hand. "*Thaumaturgical,* on the other hand, is another word for magic. What a fascinating juxtaposition, don't you think?"

Prish's solemn intent to shepherd them through a peaceable afternoon immediately dissolved in her desire to avoid another of Otra's flights of whimsy. "Who's hungry?" she asked hastily. "Should I get another hand pie to share?"

"Everyone said she was crazy," said Wick, ignoring Prish's words or too caught up in a fit of vehemence to hear them. "No one understood what she was trying to do. They called her a crackpot!" And that was where his reflexive anger rebounded against his recent changes of circumstance. He wrapped his arms around his knees and rested his forehead on them. "Maybe she was," he mumbled.

"There are worse things to be than a crackpot," suggested Otra, which Prish felt was an uncharacteristically useful thing to say right then. She hauled herself to her feet.

"Ugh! I can't sit still any longer. A bit of perambulation will do me good. Come find me when you're ready to go."

She strutted off, following the park's outer perimeter. Prish risked a glance at Wick, whose arms still hid most of his face. If Alsing had been here, she would have known exactly what to say, and how to say it. But something plainly needed to be said, and only Prish was here to do it.

"I think," she ventured, "that I'm supposed to say something along the lines of, *do you want to talk about it?* But. Well." A loose thread on the cuff of her shirt offered her a convenient option to fix her attention while she worked her way around the edge of her thoughts. "Do you want to *not* talk about it? I mean. To talk about *not it?*"

"Yes," said Wick, a bit thickly. Immediately Prish launched into several lengthy opinions about the quality of the park's foliage: The grass lawn had gone a bit patchy in places that should have had a perfectly suitable drainage situation and sun-shade ratio. Several stretches of parkland would do better if the lawn could be replaced entirely with a selection of wildflowers to attract friendly insects. "That whole stretch there," she said, indicating a long narrow expanse, "that's wasted space. Imagine a nice row of raspberries there, to eat up all that sunshine. And then people could eat up the raspberries. They hardly need any looking after, raspberries, as long as you have someone to cut back the canes in the fall to keep everything growing happy and healthy."

"I like raspberries," Wick offered, which was the first thing he'd said since she embarked on her botanical monologue.

"Well, naturally," said Prish, encouraged by this sign of life. Before she could be undone by the consequences of this mild hubris, she looked around and located Otra: still within her line of sight. Otra was intently focused on tossing a small round thing—a pebble or a marble or a bead she'd found—harmlessly up and catching it. The worst she could do was conk someone on the head. Prish could live with that, and so could whoever got pebbled. "Everyone likes raspberries. It's radishes that are a bit more unpopular."

"Too much bite," agreed Wick, and mustered a smile.

Spicy plants, of course, had evolved such flavors as a self-defense mechanism against hungry herbivores. Prish pondered how she might turn that information into some sort of life lesson, but she was forestalled by a crash of thunder and a spangle of light at the very corner of her vision.

In an instant she was on her feet. She knew that sound; she knew that light. She'd know them anywhere—anywhere except broad daylight. Her head turned wildly back and forth until she found Otra, looking back at her.

Otra pointed silently. Nearby, on a flattened patch of grass, stood a naked starstruck pill bug. His jeweled compound eyes glittered, catching the sunlight, as he gingerly felt along the lines of his antennae with his newly acquired fingers. A moment later, he was surrounded by other starstruck and a few humans as well, offering their congratulations, their greetings, their picnic blanket as a makeshift kilt. In another moment, they'd led him away.

Alsing should have been here.

"That's impossible," said Wick. "Where'd the star come from? It's not even four o'clock."

Not only was it impossible—it was the second impossible thing that had happened in Prish's vicinity in the last three days. Otra hadn't moved, watching the pill bug leave in the company of his impromptu welcome committee.

"We should go," Prish said. She pressed her hand to her chest. If she had a normal sort of heart, it would be thudding right now. She imagined she could feel the glow of her star pulsing rhythmically against her fingers. "Alsing will be wondering where we are."

The walk back to the inn, however, was put on hold as they came back through Wandleham's high streets. On the new route they followed, they found themselves on a neat little lane lined with shops owned by a grand variety of craftsfolk and artists. Otra made them stop while she peered in window after window, exclaiming over a tailor's clever stitches or the clean linework of a carpenter. Though Prish wanted to get back, even she found herself taken with the rows and rows of clocks on display in one shop, and the woven rugs hanging outside the door of another. It didn't make sense to add new possessions to the pile she already had to pull behind the bicycle, but that didn't stop her from longingly stroking the tassels of a lovely pink-and-yellow hallway runner.

"Oh, look at that!" Otra caroled, as she had approximately two dozen times in the last half hour. "A sculptor!" She shoved through the other shoppers, as Prish and Wick navigated more carefully behind her, toward a shop whose forecourt was littered with stonework of all sorts for sale. Birdbaths, grinning gargoyles, a garden bench, even some simple statuary. The proprietor himself sat on a wooden stool amid the quiet company of his wares. An older man, somewhere between going bald and already there; he had an underworked block of stone between his knees and a chisel and hammer in his hands. "Good afternoon," he called out to them, assuming, for some reason, that a radish in farm clothes, a rock in mismatched hand-me-downs, and a teenage boy would benefit from his sales pitch. "Feel free to stay and watch a spell, if you like."

"We'd love to," said Otra, bending down to inspect the angle of the stonemason's arm, before Prish could countermand her. "We're not in a rush."

Keeping the peace, Prish reminded herself. It had been a fairly good afternoon, and she hesitated to break that spell. Hopefully the innkeeper had a book that Alsing could look at, instead of worrying herself sick over where the rest of them had disappeared to. She checked on Wick, who shrugged, and settled onto the stone bench for the duration while Otra flitted around the man at his work.

Prish was not one to turn down free child-minding, especially since the sculptor seemed particularly patient with Otra's scattershot questioning—*where do you get the stone, where do they go when you've finished, what is that tool called, how do you know what this one wants to be.* She took the opportunity, with gratitude, to meander among the stonework in the forecourt, and then to duck into the shop itself. This was where the sculptor set out smaller work for display: stone vases that would fit on a sturdy side table, small statuettes for mantles, odds and ends and bits and bobs. Prish picked up a hand-sized piece that she thought, at first, was a fox, until she brought it to her eyes for closer inspection and it revealed itself to be a cat with an impressively fluffy tail. "I could get used to days like this," she told the deceptive cat. "The kind where those two aren't trying to kill each other the whole time."

As it turned out, them killing each other should not have been her main concern. A shout, a loud clack, and a congested clattering snatched Prish all at once out of her peaceful browsing. She dropped the statuette and flung herself back out the door. "What under all the good and giving skies—"

"I didn't do it!" Wick cried, and Prish had no idea what it was he had or hadn't done. He stood off to one side, both hands in the air. His eyes were wide, his face ashen.

It took Prish a moment to take in the scene, and another several moments to understand it. The stoneworker, his forehead and much of his balding pate accordion-folded with dismay, stood over a heaped pile of Otra. He had his hands up, too, and they were empty. "She asked to see," he said helplessly. "I'm so sorry. I didn't know that she would..." He gestured vaguely at his own head.

Prish hadn't known that Otra would, either, but she might have guessed. She knelt on the ground and put her weight against Otra's shoulder to roll her onto her back—despite her average frame, she was heavy, granite all the way through. The hammer fell out of her loose fingers as she moved. The chisel stayed in her other hand, trapped by the angle of her arm. A fresh chip stood out in the rough surface of her face, about halfway down, off center. A half inch or so away from the purple mark that remained of her sketched-in eye.

A pang of pity shoved its way in past Prish's outrage and alarm. "Don't you dare die on me," she commanded, arranging Otra's limbs in a fashion she hoped was more comfortable. But she wasn't even sure she would *know* if Otra had died. The stone of her face and wrists kept to the cool, ambient temperature of the air. Nor could Prish find a pulse—but who was to say if Otra had ever had one in the first place? She occupied some strange liminal place between living and—not death, perhaps, but *unlife*. "We need to get her back to the inn," she said. "Alsing will know what to do." And perhaps that was even true, but it didn't make Prish feel better to say so.

The stonemason had a cart with a ramp that slid out from its back gate. Between the three of them, they managed to drag Otra up and lay her out on a canvas tarp. As they worked, the mason repeated his apologies, and Prish repeated her assurances that there was no way he could have expected such a thing.

Wick matched Otra's stony silence for most of the ride. Only when the inn appeared around the bend of a narrow road did he venture to speak. "Is this...my fault?"

"No more than it's the sculptor's." Between them, Otra stirred for the first time, a lift of one hand that couldn't be explained away by the cart's jolting motion. Prish fussed unnecessarily with the edge of the tarp, tucking it in over Otra's side. "She would have done it regardless," she went on, shifting into a stage whisper. "Because she is who she is. We all are, obviously. Just... Otra more than most."

The cart dragged to a stop in front of the inn. Alsing sat on the front porch, nursing a cup of tea. At the sight of them in the cart, she smiled and lifted her free hand to wave. But the light in her eyes died as she took in the scene. The teacup fell out of her hand as she pushed herself up and hurried down the steps, swinging her bad leg awkwardly to the side as she went.

Wick hopped over the side of the cart before Alsing reached them. "Sometimes," he said, "I don't want to be who I am." And he disappeared up the stairs and into the door of the inn as Alsing leaned over the side of the cart, demanding explanations that Prish didn't have.

———◆———

Under Alsing's attentions, Otra roused enough to navigate—with some assistance—the stairs up to the third-floor room. After she and Alsing had disappeared around the bend of the staircase, Prish asked the innkeeper for a broom and dustpan, and took care of the broken shards of teacup that littered the porch. The weathered wood floorboards had already drunk up all the tea; hopefully the stain wouldn't be noticeable.

She offered an extra copper coin with the return of the shard-filled dustpan, in recompense for the ruined cup, but the innkeeper tutted her away. "Accidents happen," she said. "Just be more careful next time, hear?"

Which left Prish no other option but to trudge up the stairs herself. She thought about knocking at the door but found it unlocked when she tested the knob, and let herself in.

Wick huddled atop one bed, furiously pretending to read a yellowing book that had been left on the side table as decoration. He didn't look up when Prish entered, and neither did Alsing, who sat on the edge of the other bed, murmuring over Otra.

Otra, in contrast, had never learned the art of murmuring. "How can it hurt so much and be numb at the same time?" she keened, and thrashed about while Alsing struggled to hold her still. "This wasn't supposed to happen. This shouldn't ever have happened! Wick knows. Or maybe he doesn't." Wick's wide eyes peeped over the top cover of the book, then immediately fastened back onto the antique type in front of him. "But he was *supposed* to know. What happens when you end up with a destiny meant for someone else?" She kicked out and sent the ugly floral duvet flying across the room. "But if someone else already picked for me, what then? Alsing, what then? Oh, sweet skies, it *hurts*—"

The book shut with a snap. Wick rocked forward, hunched around himself. "*The mountain is my pillow,*" he sang. "*The green earth is my cloak. The mountain is my pillow, the green earth is my cloak...*"

He went on and on, cycling through those two lines, the only ones he remembered. The monotony of it seemed to soothe Otra, even as it set Prish's nerves on edge. Otra calmed enough for Alsing to throw the duvet back over her, and her flailing movements slowed.

"I think she's asleep," said Alsing softly, and Wick fell silent all at once. He deposited the book on the side table and pulled his own bedcovers over himself.

Prish and Alsing looked carefully past each other: Prish in the dark by the door, Alsing in the wan electric light from the wall fixture. "We have a long way still to go," Alsing said. She pulled up her legs, lying alongside Otra. "Get what rest you can."

"Alsing—"

"She's asleep," Alsing said, her voice small but still sharp. A needle that pierced all the way through Prish. "We'd be wise to do the same." And she rolled over, her head on the pillow, her eyes tightly shut.

Prish looked around. One bed was full of Alsing and Otra, the other had Wick knotted up in a wad of blankets to one side. She was hardly about to crawl into bed beside a child she barely knew, but for a moment, she perched on the edge of the mattress. "That was a kind thing you did just there," she said softly, for his ears only. "And the right thing, too. *Kind* and *right* don't often intersect. Always nice to follow that path for a while, though, when you find it." She patted vaguely once more; the gesture did not come naturally to her. "Maybe sometime, you should draw me a map, instead of the other way around."

"It doesn't feel that good," said Wick, muffled by the pillow and blanket. "I still don't like her very much."

"No. You're just running against the grain of selfishness a little, I suppose." She laid one hand on the lump where his shoulder should be. "Wears down smooth after a while and you don't even notice it anymore. Just part of growing up."

"What if I don't *want* it to wear all the way down?" The lump of Wick wriggled under her hand. "What if sometimes I want to do what I want?"

"Well." Prish stood up. She brushed her hands on her trousers, just to have something to do with them. "Then I guess you'd better hope life gives you a choice."

The buzz of the electric light cut itself off short when she pressed the switch and cast the room into shades of gray. "Good night," she offered, and Alsing's ears flicked once.

A small armchair had been shoved into one corner of the room. Prish slouched into it, stretching her legs out as far as the space would allow, and tucked her chin onto her chest. Not that much worse than sleeping on the cold hard ground, she told herself. But at least she hadn't had to sleep there alone.

———◆———

Come the morning, Prish slunk out of the room before the others had stirred—she'd barely slept in the chair as it was, and carrying a tray of tea and bacon and toast up two flights of stairs seemed as good an addition as any to her penance. By the time she eased the door open, Alsing sat blearily upright, and Wick brushed past her out the door, muttering something about the toilet.

"Good morning," said Prish, sounding a bit desperate, if she was honest with herself.

But Alsing mustered a smile—albeit with clear effort—and a greeting in kind. "Good morning. That smells nice."

"Cinnamon tea and something to fill our bellies for the road." She set the tray down on the side table and poured hot water from the pot into a pair of teacups. "Milk or sugar?"

"Oh, don't be disgusting," said Alsing, and the smile looked a bit more genuine as she took her cup to submerge the tea strainer.

The bed bounced and she nearly splashed herself with water as Otra sat bolt upright behind her. "Good morning, good morning!" Otra said brightly, who by all indications seemed to have bounced straight back to her usual manic good cheer. Apparently rocks could benefit from a sound night's rest as much as anyone else could. "Oh—may I?" She snatched a piece of bacon off the plate and plastered it to her face in a greasy approximation of a grin. "What do you think?"

"I think you shouldn't waste perfectly good food," Prish objected, then quickly corrected herself: "But it's not as if such soggy bacon qualifies as *perfectly good* food anyway, so you may as well leave it."

Otra beamed—or at least the bacon's upward curve made it look as if she was. "It's going to be a good day," she said. "Oh, that's a relief, isn't it?"

By the time Wick returned from the facilities, they had doled out the rest of the bacon and the toast into three equal portions. They took careful bites and made careful conversation. No one said anything about Wick's song or Prish's guilt or the new dent in Otra's face. There were a few moments when Prish thought Alsing might broach one of those difficult subjects, but she never did, and if she wasn't going to, Prish would certainly follow her lead. This brittle peace had been hard won, and so they handled it gently. If they were lucky, Prish thought, it would carry them the rest of the way to the Midland Lows. But then again Prish had never been the sort of radish who invested much in the idea of luck.

✦

They took a much more subdued walk out of the city than they'd had arriving. No one pointed out the sights, and no one begged to visit this attraction or that. No one offered to buy anyone else any sort of food sold on a stick. *Warm day for autumn,* someone would say, and someone else would agree. *How far do you suppose we'll get today? Oh, fifteen miles, maybe less, it gets hilly from here. Do you want me to take a turn on the bike? No, no, I'm fine for a spell yet, thanks.*

On the road north, they met nearly as many fellow travelers as they had on the way into Wandleham—but most of these were headed in the opposite direction. Not much to do except offer a passing greeting. No one to talk to but each other. And nothing worthwhile to say.

Soon the hills rose up under their feet. "They're called the Crestway," Prish told Wick, just to have something new to say. And even if they were only hills, they felt rather like the mountains in Wick's little song. Prish watched Alsing's limp worsen as the day went on. She folded up all the worries and solicitous questions she would have said and made them small and put them away to deal with on her own later. Alsing would not want to be minded by her right now, and anyway she'd already very recently and spectacularly proved her lack of ability in the field of minding.

Otra, too, refused any efforts to check in on her current state. She seemed to have left the worst effects of the previous day behind, though she walked a bit behind the others, and fostered fewer attempts at conversation (or at monologues of wild fancy). Whenever Alsing offered a chance to rest, she demurred. "Places to go," she said. "People to see." The bacon fell off her face at some point, unnoticed, and undoubtedly made the day of some very lucky raven or vole.

By the time the sun was making its bed on the horizon, they had climbed to the heights of the Crestway, and Wick was the first to cry out when he spotted the blanket of deep, dark sea spread out to the west. He ran ahead, with Otra trotting close after, while Prish pushed the bike stubbornly upward alongside Alsing (she had given up on pedaling until she could enjoy a bit of downhill again).

They caught up to the other two where they'd stopped at the bend of a hairpin turn, staring out over the water. "Very pretty," said Alsing, and lifted one claw to point out the sun's colors bleeding into one another in the wet place where the sky met the sea. "Do you know—I don't believe I've ever seen the sea before."

"Where would we have?" Prish traced their life together back through her memories: the city, the cabin in the Craftwood, the road to the Midland Lows. "First time for everything, my darling."

"And a last time," said Otra in a muddy voice. She shifted, straightening her shoulders, and cocked her head at Alsing. "The last first time you'll see the sea. How sad!"

"Can we go closer?" Wick pleaded. "I've never seen it before either."

Prish glanced at Alsing, who shrugged. "It's getting late," she said. "We may as well leave the path to find someplace suitable to sleep."

"Yes," Otra said. "This is as good a place as any. I'd like it very much." She twisted her fingers together, clicking and clacking. "Stopping here."

Well, if the Midland Lows weren't getting any closer tonight anyway... They came down the westerly face of the hill, choosing their footfalls with great discretion. It took longer, avoiding the steepest slopes, but they came around the side of another hill, lower and nearer the water, and on its side stood a little cottage.

The windows were dark, not a glimmer of candles, though it was too late to cook or read or sew without added light, and too early for sensible folk to go to bed. "Maybe they're away," said Prish.

"No," said Alsing. "I don't think so. But we'll knock anyway. Why not?"

But before Prish could set her fist to the door, Otra tested the knob, which turned in her hand. "Hello?" she called, putting one hand up to the smear of bacon grease that lingered. She stepped inside, her head swinging back and forth. "Is anybody home?"

Nobody was, and nobody had been for quite some time. A thin layer of dust curled up into the air to mark their passage through empty rooms or up empty stairs. The larder was bare, the drawers in the upstairs rooms empty—except for one bureau. When Prish opened it, she found children's clothing and women's boots, men's trousers in half a dozen sizes, a hand-knit sweater of indistinct shape, three different styles of hat. It felt dreadfully familiar and strange all at the same time.

"Do you think..." she asked Alsing, who had followed her into the upstairs bedroom. "Do you think that whoever lived here—did what we did?"

Alsing looked at the child's blouse and the pair of extra-large trousers that Prish held up in each hand. "I think," she said slowly, "that they're gone now, and it doesn't much matter what they were, or who." And she retreated out into the hall in a flash of white-tipped tail.

Where a stove should have stood, they found only a discolored patch of floor and a pipe hanging sadly out of the ceiling. Still, they had enough provisions that would tolerate being eaten cold. Wick went out to a small bench that sat in front of the house, shoulders pulled up tight against the cool breeze off the water as he ate; Prish and Alsing contented themselves with the glass-blurred view from the window.

They both stood partway up out of their seats when Otra swanned toward the door, announcing her intentions to explore a bit. "Oh, don't look at me like that," she said, dismissing them with a *shoo-shoo* gesture. "There aren't any chisels in evidence, and if it makes you feel better, I solemnly swear that I won't put another mark in my face by any other means, either."

"A few minutes' stroll, then." Alsing settled back into her seat with an audible *oof*. "Please understand that we're just worried about you. That's all."

"I understand more than you think," said Otra, with wounded pride. But she paused, smoothing down the wrinkled front of her sweater. "Thank you, Alsing. I do appreciate all the worrying, even if I haven't been good about showing it. I want you to know that."

"Don't you try to sweet-talk me," said Alsing, teasing but firm. "A few minutes, do you hear?"

"Of course." If Otra had eyes, Prish suspected she would have rolled them then. "Good evening, ladies."

They caught a glimpse of her, a smudge of purple and white and gold, wending her way around the side of the hill. Outside, she exchanged a few words with Wick as she went, but the wind rubbed away any distinguishing characteristics of what was said.

A fragile quiet settled in, gentle clinks and clacks of cutlery against plate and cups against table. Prish scraped up the last few crumbs with one finger, then adjusted the alignment of her fork where it rested on her plate. "Good to see Otra up and around," she said. "Back to her usual self a little."

There was a long, deliberate silence as Alsing took a bite of cheese, chewed it, and swallowed. "It should never have happened, Prish."

"*I* didn't put the chisel in her hand!" The plate jumped as Prish barked her knees against the underside of the table. A few dented, gray-green peas bounced over the plates rim and onto the tablecloth. "I didn't want it to happen either. I wish it hadn't. Otra rubs me the wrong way sometimes, sure, but I've never wished to see another person in pain, not once. That's not me. You know that, don't you? Sweet and sacred skies, I hope you know that by now." The words came out of her, the seal she'd put between them and Alsing broken and nothing left to stopper the rest up. "If I could have stopped it, I would have. But I'm really not sure I could have, not once she'd gotten that particular bee in her bonnet. It's not as if I get a lot of say in what does or doesn't happen around here."

The words landed between them much more heavily than the peas had, and there was no nudging them back into place with a spoon.

"Say what you really mean." A furious round of flicking seized Alsing's ears. "What kind of—of agency have I been denying you?"

"*I never wanted to leave in the first place.*"

Too late, Prish realized she'd shouted. Alsing's ears had flattened along the back of her skull. "You never told me that," Alsing said quietly. "How could I have known?"

It was exactly that quiet surprise that sent the righteous anger that Prish had been privately stoking all along into a rapid simmer. She slapped both hands down on either side of her plate, sending her fork skittering. "You knew we'd built a life there. You knew all the hours—the years!—I'd spent on the garden, and the house." Cool, calm reason shredded when she tried to pull it back around herself. She held the scraps close. "But when you said it would hurt you to stay there, what was I supposed to say, except *yes, darling, of course, darling?*"

"You were supposed to tell me the truth." A flash of white teeth as Alsing's lips pulled back around the words. Sharp, but not as sharp as what she said, or the way she said it. "You were supposed to talk to me, not expect me to read your thoughts."

"And *you* were supposed to—" The rage had boiled away, and left some unpleasant stains on the kettle she'd kept it in. She pushed back from the table and stood in the middle of the living room, unsure where to go now, too tired to pace back and forth without a destination in mind. "You never asked. So maybe you didn't really want to know in the first place."

Alsing exhaled hard, and she slouched forward, as if everything that held her upright had broken all at once. Her ears had stopped twitching now, and her brow rested against the pane of the window. "I suppose," she said, "it doesn't do much good to say now that I'm sorry."

"You haven't said it." Prish put her hands in her pockets, then took them out. The dirty dishes still lay on the table; gathering them up gave her something to do, and she did it. "So I can't really say."

Alsing didn't call after her when she carried the dishes to the kitchen, scrubbed them aggressively with a pump of tepid water from the sink, swiped them slightly drier and shoved them back into the nearest cupboard. When she returned to the sitting room, Alsing still sat with her head against the window. "Prish," she said, and her tone was the closest thing to an apology that Prish expected to get. "It's been more than a few minutes. I'd go myself, but..."

"It's fine," Prish said, knowing that this was also the closest thing to an apology that she expected to offer. "I'll go find her."

———◆———

Prish set out from the cabin on a vaguely circular path, expanding out in wider spirals through the trees when Otra didn't turn up right away. Worrying about Otra did not come naturally to her, but in light of recent events, she found herself more than up to the task, especially as she called Otra's name over and over without response. Images of Otra shattered on the rocky shoreline below forced themselves gruesomely into her thoughts, and she walked faster, then pushed herself to a jog.

When she found Otra perched on a half-rotted bench along a cliffside path, though, annoyance muted her relief. "Didn't you hear me calling?" she said, putting her hands on her knees to catch her breath. "The sound from the waves isn't *that* loud."

"Oh, dear," said Otra. She fidgeted with something in her lap. "I should have been a bit faster, I think. I'm sorry. It's hard, you know?"

"I do not in the least know." Prish straightened up enough to make a come-along gesture. "You can explain more tomorrow. It's late, and we should get back." The restless movement of Otra's hands drew her attention. Was that a glass jar? That funny little leather case from Wick's house lay on the ground by her feet, too, open and empty. "What's that you've got there? You don't eat jam, so if you've been wasting our supplies—!"

"It's my supply to waste," Otra interrupted. "And I've tried not to waste it, I really have. I've tried all these days!" The fidgeting intensified; Prish caught another glimpse of the object, which also had a complicated-looking apparatus attached. "And that might not seem very long for someone who is, technically, thousands of years old. But it is a very long time for someone who is also, well, *only all these days* old. It's a very long time, when you can feel everything and nothing at the same time, all the time, always."

Prish had had enough time to catch her breath by now, but urgency drew it tight and short again. She didn't know what Otra was talking about, but she knew she didn't like it. "That's enough out of you, all right? We're going to go find Alsing and get you settled in for the night. With someone sitting on you, if we have to, to keep you from another one of these walkabouts!"

"Wick's mum and dad were up to something," Otra said, peeling off full speed onto a complete perpendicular. "But I don't think it agreed with them. It doesn't agree with me. And I certainly don't agree with it." She held up the device: it was small, and the apparatus Prish had seen before connected the jar and a small bell-shaped aperture, which looked as if it had been purloined from a miniature phonograph. Before she could ask again about it, Otra pressed on. "That's why they're gone, you see. It was too much for them to hold. He can follow them if he wants to, but I really don't think you should let him."

"What's too much? Where did they go?" Prish threw her hands up in the air. "And I have no idea why you think I get to decide who's allowed to do what! Everyone does what they want around here, and they leave me to clean up the mess!"

"One more mess, then," Otra said sadly. "Sorry about that. I'm going to go now, Prish. I'm sorry I was always terrible."

"Go where? Is this about your destiny again, or—?"

Instead of answering, Otra flicked a switch on the apparatus. Or perhaps that was an answer in itself. The device flashed so brightly that it scorched a layer of color off Prish's vision; when she blinked away the spangles in her eyes, Otra no longer sat on the bench.

The path was empty, too. Prish rushed to the edge of the cliff, searching the seaside below. But there was no splash of orange and purple to be seen on the rocks, no smashed pile of stone. Nothing. It was like Otra had simply ceased to be.

She turned back to the bench. The device lay on its side where Otra had dropped it. When Prish picked it up, a single marble, glowing brightly, bounced at the bottom of the jar.

Beneath where the device had rested, a dinner plate–sized slab of slate sat on the bench.

Prish set the device carefully aside. The stone was cool when she touched it, the same temperature as the night air. She lifted it carefully, holding it tightly, as if that would still the shaking of her hands. Her fingers slid along the underside and found a single deep chip along the edge.

"Prish?"

She clutched the stone to her chest as she spun. Alsing emerged around the side of the cliff, leaning on Wick's arm. "You told me to handle it," Prish said, because she needed to say something and could not put the rest of her thoughts to words, nor even to sense.

"Then you should have handled it with less shouting." Though Alsing said this the same way that they always exchanged gentle teasing, it landed more heavily with the weight of their previous conversation to drive it home. She let go of Wick's arm as he kept walking toward Prish. "Where's Otra?"

"I didn't—" The chip in the stone bit into Prish's finger when she gripped it tighter. She didn't have blood, but sap trickled down the back of her hand, her wrist. "I couldn't stop her." She hadn't even understood what she was trying to stop. She still didn't, not quite, though the pieces scraped together inside her head, begging to fit together. "Alsing..."

But it was Wick who spoke. "She said mine would be here soon." His voice sounded funny, faraway. He had picked up the device, watching the marble roll back and forth along the jar's curve. "She said I would understand soon."

"What did Otra say?" Alsing demanded. "Did you know about—about this?"

But he didn't mean Otra, Prish realized. *She said*: his mother's note. The pieces jarred together faster now, chipping away rough edges. Forming a blurry mosaic, like a picture seen through an antique window. The full jar of identical marbles in Wick's house. The device. Wick's abnormal focus now, the way the light from that single marble reflected in his eyes. Two parents who had disappeared at the drop of a hat. *Starstruck are so entitled*, he'd parroted, and perhaps not from the schoolyard at all. A pair of natural philosophers, or crackpots, depending on who you asked, who'd lived in the woods for a year or two now or maybe somewhere in the middle of that. Stars that had stopped falling— or at least that had stopped falling where anyone else might find them. One single star that, perhaps pulled off course, had fallen quite unexpectedly onto a rock, and another onto a stray pill bug.

A series of unconnected and impossible things that were all, actually, the same thing down at the core of it. What if you wanted magic of your own, and what if you looked out at a world of talking radishes and foxes and pill bugs and even rocks and thought to yourself, *well, why shouldn't some of that be mine*? "Wick," she whispered, her chest too tight to yell. "Don't."

Because what kind of magic was a star but a trembling, living soul—and who, who could safely hold a second soul? No one. Not a starstruck, Prish thought, and not a human being, however they might try. However dearly they might desire it, and the lie of power they'd told themselves about it.

And what would happen to someone who did? Would it burn her from the inside out? Would it change him into something that could no longer be held in a human shape? What about a snippet of song that refused to be forgotten? What about a new color in the night sky?

"Someone needs to tell me what's going on," Alsing insisted, and Wick began to unscrew the jar from the device.

"No!" Prish grabbed his arm. "Wick, please, you can't. It'll destroy you! Just like it did to her!"

"This one is for me." A note of whining pierced into his naked desire. "She *promised*."

"Stop fighting!" Alsing tried to push her way between them. "You're both behaving like—"

Wick wrenched free of Prish's grasp, but the device clipped Alsing's arm and spun out of his hands. It arced through the air, and Prish grabbed for it, and Wick did, too, and there was a flash of golden light—

———◆———

When Wick's vision clears, he's on his hands and knees. He blinks, looking around, and catches a flash of white as it vanishes along the cliffside path. Or maybe that's just the stars in his eyes?

The stars—

He grabs the device where it's fallen. The jar broke open where it fell on an ugly chunk of rock; Wick tosses the jagged glass aside and brushes away loose dirt from an uprooted plant that's tangled amid the shards. And there they are: three tiny spheres that click together in his palm when he grabs them out of the scrubby grass.

Round, glittering, alight from the inside. Two are perfect as polished gems, not a flaw to be seen, smooth where they meet his fingertips. His mouth waters when he touches them. He thinks he can hear them singing: the music of the spheres, the tongue that only magic can teach. His parents weren't *crackpots. They didn't abandon him; they were only going on ahead, forging the path for him to follow. And what a beautiful path it is! It will take him and carry him impossibly far forward.* Pick me, *the marbles insist.* Pick me and I will make you so much more than what you are now. No, pick me—

The third marble is cracked from its impact on the stone slab. What light lingers inside is already foundering. A sense of dismay cuts into his joy, his desire. This marble was his friend. Is. Or it should be. No more. Whatever meaning these spheres were supposed to hold was gone.

Or maybe just elsewhere. For a moment.

Until someone calls it back.

That was a kind thing you did, *says Prish's voice in his head, and adds, in an altogether different tone:* Then you'd better hope life gives you a choice. *That's exactly what life has given him and he's more hopeless than ever. People who loved him and left him; people he'd known less than a week. It's hardly a choice at all. Is it?*

He turns the device over and over in his hands. His mother designed something to snatch up stars, and his father built it. Stars. Souls. Magic. Something. It's not really murder, *if you think about it. It's misdirection. A mistake. That fox is still running around here somewhere. That radish's roots will take in new soil. The rock—*

"*The mountain is my pillow,*" *Wick sings, and it's like feeling his mother's hand on his shoulder. She's so close. Impossibly close, and she's been there all along, he* understands now, threading her way through his thoughts, never out of reach. So she didn't really leave him at all! And now he can be just as close to her, in turn.

He just has to choose.

Three marbles—but no, the cracked one is already fading. He wonders whose it was, whose it was supposed to be. He looks around and sees a glimmer that might have been a pair of amber eyes, a purple gash showing through green skin, a pale gray facet that wasn't quite a face. He's already lost one—he's already losing her—and he doesn't know how to stop it, or fix it. Who could?

Except. Except one person, fooling around in the park. Tossing a pebble in the air and catching it; tossing a pebble in the air and letting a pill bug catch it instead. What goes up—it must go down, and so too must his choice.

"Tell me what to do." His voice cracks, but the little glowing spheres are still and lifeless, impervious to his begging. If they move at all, it's only borrowed energy from the trembling of his hands. They should be hot to the touch, he thinks. They should hurt to hold. They sing his name in the sweetest tones he's ever heard, and he wants to swallow them whole, he wants them to swallow him.

He gropes along the ground, half-seeing. Broken glass bites into his hand, but he doesn't care. Even knowing what he knows, even feeling what he feels, he can't look away from the glow of the marbles, he can't close his ears to their call. He finds the tangle of roots; he finds the glass-shattering face of rock.

His fist closes around the three marbles. Even still, he realizes, he will have to choose.

The fox is gone, long gone. So that's one terrible choice made for him. "Come back!" he shouts after her, but foxes have never had much call to heed the demands of human boys. His voice breaks before he can call again, and he falls flat on the ground, curled around the marbles. Great choking sobs give way to dry heaving, and he holds the marbles to his chest, the broken one closest of all. Why can't anyone ever just stay with him? Why can't anyone just stay?

By the time tears subside, his resolve hasn't so much solidified as congealed. He pushes it up from the depths of his heart, and it grates unkindly over the selfish urge to steal a star, to swallow a soul, to follow where he shouldn't. When it passes, it leaves things a little smoother than it found them, and he knows it'll be a little easier the next time, and the time after that. It won't be easy to tell the difference, between when it's time to choose for himself and when it's time to choose for others. But he can see that learning how to make space between the two is part of growing up.

Radishes can be wrong as often as right, however much you like them. And rocks can get some things right, annoying though they may be. And foxes—

He looks around for a glimpse of white fur, and finds none.

He's the only one who can choose, though he still fears what comes next. He can't tell them apart, one from the next, not like this. He doesn't even know which one is broken (though he can hope; oh, sweet skies, he can hope with all his guilty heart). If he guesses wrong, nothing good will happen. Nothing right. Nothing that deserves a second chance.

"Just come back," he pleads again. But there's no one left to hear him. "Please." And he throws them all, shining through a smear of blood, up into the air.

The broken marble lands heavily in front of him. The other two seem to linger a moment in the air. Then they, too, drive home: this time with a flash of brilliant light.

———◆———

The walls of the seaside cottage were all but covered with paintings, outside and in.

Afternoon shadows followed Prish up onto the porch. She opened the door and peered inside, letting her eyes adjust to the light. They'd moved some of the furniture around, but mostly they'd been content to leave it as the previous inhabitants had arranged it. The walls were where they'd made the place truly *theirs*: swimming with artwork, with heavy branched pine forests and cityscapes and eerie underwater tableaux, with stars and moons and suns. The faces of friends and strangers alike peeped out from between still lifes of pitchers and harvested crops.

Prish stopped to rest a moment against the doorjamb before she went in. Sometimes just walking into the house was more than she could bear. The only thing worse would have been to walk away from it entirely. She shifted the day's catch of fish on her shoulder and wondered what would happen when there was no more wall space to be had. Perhaps they'd have to whitewash over it all again to give Otra somewhere fresh to work.

Once Prish had shaken the sand from her boots, she went inside to find Otra perched atop a table in the kitchen, her neck canted back to paint on the ceiling. "Oh, you're back early today, aren't you?" She dabbed with the brush and nodded her approval of the result. "He's around back, if that's who you're looking for. I can't imagine who else you'd expect to find in the house, anyway."

"I'm looking for anyone who's going to help me clean and gut these fish." Prish's pant legs were still heavy with damp; heavy enough to drag on the bare boards of the floor. But there was no one to scold her or send her to change into something dryer. The flesh of her legs felt desiccated, sucked dry by the greedy salt in the water. She took the measure of that sensation, filed it away for consideration. "Must I keep us fed all on my own? Or are you going to earn your keep today?"

"My keep!" Otra snorted. "I'm far less trouble to have around than either of you two, with your constant needs for fresh water and food and air and light. What's a little bit of paint compared to all that?" But she climbed down from the table and left the paintbrush and palette behind. She tugged the gloves free from her hands—white, supple artificers' gloves, dappled with a hundred different colors of paint now—and set them aside in favor of a rougher pair that she produced from one pocket. Her face was spattered liberally with paint droplets too: if there was any remnant of a chalk-sketched face beneath it all, Prish could not make it out. "Let's take care of this, then, before this mess gets to smelling any worse. I imagine it does smell foul? Only I haven't the sense of smell to tell on my own. Also, stop picking at that scar or it will never properly heal."

Prish took her hand away from the raised brownish line drawn across her forehead and left eyebrow. "Sorry," she said unapologetically. Sometimes she thought she wanted to have a wound that wouldn't quite heal, and sometimes she thought the itching would drive her fully mad. Otra heaved a theatrical sigh. Together, they dragged the table outside and worked side by side. The knives that had been left in the kitchen drawers were dull but functional. The same way Prish felt now.

Seabirds darted in here and there, rustling in the long grass outside the cabin door as they risked proximity on the chance of a free fish head or two. Occasionally there was a glimmer of movement from the next lean-to down the hill, where a recently starstruck gull had set up a little home of his own, halfway between a house and a nest. He was unloading a pile of branches he'd carried out of the woods, probably to strengthen the roof they'd helped him build. When Prish stood up straight to stretch her back, he raised a hand in greeting. She echoed the gesture. Didn't hurt anything to be gracious, she thought, and that lie prickled her.

"Well! That's that, then, I suppose." Otra gathered up the stained, dented knives. "One more thing checked off in the never-ending checklist of keeping the lot of you alive." The slab of slate tilted skyward, where pink fingers waited on the horizon to catch the setting sun. "I suppose it's getting on to be time? I'll wash these off and scrub the table if you want to, ah. Take care of everything."

"Thank you." The words ground out of Prish more easily than they had, at the start of this new and different and salt-bitter life. But they still ground out, crumbled and chipped at the edges. She put her head down, so that the tangle of her leaves hid her face, and gathered up the bucket of fish.

Half of the catch stayed in the cold-water bucket, while Prish set the cook-fire for the night's supper in the wood-burning stove Otra had haggled from a passing peddler for a painted portrait on the side of his wagon. Pictures and sweet words went a long way with starstruck when, as rumor had it, you were the one who had brought stars back into the world. There had to be something special about the only starstruck rock in the world, didn't there? Prish was happy enough to let Otra wrap herself in that particular glory. Maybe it had been her destiny all along. It was a rather small destiny, to be in the right place at the right time to break a jar, but Otra seemed content enough with it. Other things had been destroyed that day, and Prish knew that those millstones belonged around her neck and hers alone.

The remainder of the fish went into a salt box to cure and keep for the days when the sea was not so generous— or rather, the remainder but one. The last fish went into a dented, scratched tin pan, which Prish carried outside and around the back of the house.

Wick sat there, his back against the wall. She hoped the paint had dried on that particular spot, but so many of their clothes now bore blotches and spots of red and blue and purple that perhaps it didn't entirely matter. She had taken up so many odd and idle bits of worrying, these past two or three weeks. It felt as if somebody should.

The boy looked up at the crunch of her boots on the sand, and he started guiltily. "Prish! I brought down some water for drinking, and mucked out the chamber pot, and—" He glanced over her wet, gore-streaked clothes, and at the tin pan in her hands. "I'm too late to help with dinner, I guess."

"I guess." She walked out several paces into the deep grass and settled the pan into a bit of a bare spot. Then she retreated to the cabin, to Wick's side. "How's it coming along?"

His hands had darted to cover up the scribbled papers on his lap, but he eased them back now at her question. The cut on his hand had healed, a long pucker of white skin across the heel of his palm. He told her it didn't hurt anymore, and she mostly believed him. "I don't know. Nothing ever seems to fit quite right."

She sat down beside him. Her hands were too empty, so empty they ached. She let her arms rest on her knees and tried to scrape the words out of the empty barrel at her center. "Sometimes there's no cure for that but one. Nothing but time. Time to let the rough edges wear down." He didn't look at her, but his lips pursed out, and his dark hair fell forward into his eyes so she couldn't see them anymore. She brushed his long bangs back and let her hand stay behind on his head. "Come on. Let me hear what you've got so far."

He licked his lips and tentatively raised his voice:
"The mountain is my pillow,
The green earth is my cloak.
The moon is my guide homeward,
The stars will greet me there."

His voice faded on the last note. It was a good voice, strong and clear. Not a man's voice, not yet, though very nearly there. He blinked, as the song drifted away from them, and ducked his head under Prish's hand in embarrassment. "It's stupid."

"I like it. And I expect Otra will, too." She nodded, and her head tapped rhythmically against the wall behind her. Otra had liked every attempt that Wick had made so far at giving the song a proper ending. *It deserves the fullness of its being,* she would often say. *We all do. You should try it sometime, it's marvelous.* "You should keep trying, if you're not satisfied with it yet. But yes. I like it."

"It's just the chorus," he muttered. "There's still verses to write, and—"

"Wick!"

The cry came from some distance. Prish sat forward and looked down toward the shoreline: Otra's tiny figure flitted about among the rocks down there, no longer cleaning the fish knives but filling her apron with polished stones and bits of shell and who knew what other rubbish. So who had called?

When she turned her head to the left again, Wick was on his feet, staring up the gentle slope of the sandy grassland. "Kailenn," he said, and his voice cracked and shattered into a thousand delicate pieces. "Kailenn!"

And he was gone, racing up the hill in a great spray of sand. The round, red-faced woman chasing the dusk down the hill toward him caught him in a tangle of arms and glad cries, and the sturdily built lady who huffed up just behind her grabbed them both in her massive arms and swung them both around like children's dolls.

Well. So that was that.

The house would be a bit quieter now. And one fewer mouth to feed. Prish rubbed her knotted knuckles into the shallow dents of her eyes. She was tired, that was all, and this would be a bit less of a burden. A good end for everyone involved. Except Otra, maybe. She would miss the boy's songs.

The tall grass rustled—not up the hill, but around the tin plate that she'd left to sit out. The fox that stood half in, half out of the plate to gobble its meal had gone entirely gray about the muzzle, and her limp had only grown worse over the weeks. Not long left now, Prish thought, and then wished she could rip her heart from her breast and such traitorous thoughts along with it. "I'll be here," she said. The fox's ears pricked, though she did not look up from her supper. "I'll be here."

The last morsels of fish disappeared into the fox's hungry maw. Her head came up, amber eyes flashing across Prish. Her tail lifted, and she vanished in a soft rain of sand on tin.

"Prish?" The boy had come back, his family in tow. Prish made herself stand and shook the sand and grass free from her clothes. Might as well be presentable. "Prish, these are my cousins, Kailenn and Ismene."

The round woman—Kailenn—squashed tears away from her cheeks. Prish hadn't gotten any better at guessing human ages in the past few weeks, but she put Kailenn somewhere in young adulthood, older than Wick by several years and younger than Prish by roughly the same amount. "Prish. I understand I've got you to thank for—for everything."

"Not just me. Mostly not me at all, really. I just happened to be there." The wrong place at the wrong time. "He told you what happened?"

"In his letter." Kailenn's smile suffered a little for its wear. Behind her, Ismene jutted her jaw forward and glared up at the sky, as if that would disguise the wet tracks that shone like comets on her cheeks. "I'm sorry."

"Me, too," said Prish. She offered Kailenn her hand, and Kailenn accepted, grasping her fingers tightly. Strong hands, that one. Prish appreciated folks with strong hands. Strong hands were those that hadn't been long idle. She was a baker, Wick had said, while writing the letter to his family, telling them where to find him.

When Kailenn let go, it was to gather Wick tightly against her side. "I know we don't know you at all," she said haltingly. "And you don't know us. But if this place is—too hard for you—you'd be welcome to join us in the Lows. There's always need for those who know their way around fields and fertilizer."

Wick looked up at Prish, his eyes hard with the kind of hope that lay over a deep, dark hurt. His longing was so heavy it made her lean toward him: he was a sun whose gravity struggled to pull her closer, and she was only a moon blasted out of the orbit of her own dear world. Otra would go gladly enough, if she was asked, and he was just a boy still, one who needed very much to know that he was loved...

Prish smiled at him but shook her head slowly. A little movement of her head, and it was one of the hardest things she'd ever done. Above them, a single star sparked across the sky—not chasing the sun toward the sea but driving hard inward. Prish tore her eyes away from watching where it would land.

"We'll visit," she said. "More often than you would like, probably."

She watched a single ray of relief shine through Wick's sorrow, and let it light her up just a little. More than she deserved. Above the treetops, a streak of gold blazed up and bled just as quickly away. Otra's delighted cry barely reached her ears above the wind in the branches and the sea's constant sighs.

"It's not to say this place isn't hard. But we've put a good bit of work into it already. And there's enough room for a garden on the leeward side of the house. You know, in the spring." She put her hands in her pockets and rocked back on her heels, noting the indescribable color of the waves at this time of the evening—blue and gold and orange and purple and yet also absolutely none of those things at all. "I think I could learn to love a place like this. Given a just a little bit of time."

ACKNOWLEDGMENTS

Just like the beauty heart radish that inspired it, this book sprouted small and grew into what it is because a lot of people were involved in creating the conditions necessary for it to thrive. Robyn Bennis, who was kind enough to read an early draft of this book back when it was a young adult novel not long after we met in 2016 and who has believed in it fervently ever since, even during the periods where I did not. Martha Wells and Gregory Wilson, whose praise and thoughtful criticism on that early draft helped me on the path to this final version. Summer Fletcher, who provided great feedback on the YA draft, as well as Bennett North, who also helped with the interminable process of writing a query letter. The roots of this book reach far back and I'm grateful for all the places they found purchase.

My writing community, all you lovely people whose support I have so valued and who I admire so much every day I sit down to read your words, you are the water that quenches the dry dusty soil of my brain: Eugenia Triantafyllou, Jennifer Hudak, Kaitlyn Zivanovich, Simone Heller, and everyone in my Anxiety Coven.

The wonderful team at Psychopomp and everyone else involved in working on and alongside this project, helping tend to this little bookish crop: Sean Markey, E. Catherine Tobler, Melissa Ren, Felicia Martínez, Cory Skerry, Josephine Stewart, John G. Reinhart, Christine M. Scott, and the band Hail Your Highness.

And last but never least: my spouse, my children, you are my sunshine. Because of your light and your warmth, all of this is possible.

The summer my grandmother disappeared, taking an entire Texas town with her, she showed me photos of her ghosts.

She placed the photos on the kitchen counter, snapping each one against the shell-pink Formica like playing cards. Some of the more interesting ones she tapped with her finger to make sure I took special notice. "That one there was taken out near Sterling City."

"You took it?"

"No, a woman lives there took it. Sent it to me."

It was a Polaroid with *Thanksgiving 1978* written along the bottom. A little girl with a long-sleeve shirt and blue jeans tucked into red cowboy boots sat in a high-backed wicker chair, laughing, and pointing back at the camera. Blue light blossomed out from behind the chair in a vaguely humanoid shape, and two tendrils wrapped around the girl like transparent arms, giving her a hug.

"Lady who sent this say the girl is her daughter, and the ghost is her late mother.. She died that summer before. The old woman used to favor that chair. Her ghost started making a whole lot of racket around the house anytime somebody sat in it. This was a few years back, so might be she's moved along by now."

"What kind of racket?"

"Oh, just knocking on walls and stomping around. I recorded it. It's on one of my cassettes."

I wasn't sure I wanted to hear it. The thought of dying and being bound to the real world while everyone carried on around you was more frightening to me than the ghosts themselves. If I had to die, I figured I'd rather go someplace else.

Granny filled an ashtray full of lipstick-stained cigarette butts while we talked our way through her stack of photos. Some she'd taken herself, others she'd received from people familiar with her reputation. Most of the photos showed smiling people with circular splotches above their heads, or streaks of light cutting across the image. Maybe the camera captured a bug. Maybe it was a trick of the light. Others were harder to explain, like the crying woman floating above a glassy lake, draped in a long white dress, arms outstretched.

Granny put down a second photo of the same floating woman, same position, like it was taken immediately after the first, except this time the woman's dress was stained a deep red and she had the head of a horse. Her body was soft around the edges, like the camera had moved before the image could resolve.

"This one shows La Llorona. You remember the story I told you?"

"Yes, I know that one." I stared at the picture. The horse woman's lips were curled back around her flat teeth in a way that made it look like she was smiling.

"Might not ought to show you some of these."

"Why not?"

"They're liable to keep you up with nightmares."

"Can I see the ones they took here?"

"Let's save those for another time."

Various people had taken photos in Granny's house, both before and after she moved here, and she kept them in a cigar box in her desk, stacks of them bound with rubber bands. She'd always been happy to show me the rest of her photo collection, no matter how terrifying, but so far, she'd never been inclined to show me those in the cigar box.

I wasn't sure why she thought they would frighten me more than the others. More than her house itself.

The place was thoroughly haunted.

That's why she'd moved there in the first place.

Ghosts bled out from the margins of that old house, and I made friends with a few of them. Like thin gray memories they clung to the undersides of coffee tables and dwelled in the narrow space between the guest bed and the wall. In the nighttime, I'd peer over the edge of the mattress at their dull forms and whisper my secrets to them. They wouldn't respond, but I judged their interest in the way their eyes never wavered from mine.

In the daylight they were like half-erased pencil marks against the windows and the walls, often escaping notice and more easily forgotten, but still grasping at whatever reality they called their own.

Among my favorites was the ghost of a girl about my age whom I'd decided to call Shirley. She wore an old-style dress I couldn't place in time, and she lingered at my grandmother's bookshelves, drawing the outline of her fingertips across the spines of the books. The raspy sound of her fingers running against the paperbacks was the only noise she ever made. When she settled on one,

I'd read it aloud to her. Frequently it would be *We Have Always Lived in the Castle*, but today it was *Something Wicked This Way Comes*, and I believe she picked this one because I'd told her it was my favorite.

We passed most mornings this way, me a pudgy boy in beat-up tennis shoes and brown corduroys, my hair buzzed down in what they used to call a summer cut, and her, little more than a silver outline of the person she used to be, but with blue eyes that had never entirely released their hold on life.

My grandmother often watched us from the doorway; Granny was wraith-thin and hollowed by cancer, a wreath of cigarette smoke spinning over her head. She was only in her mid-fifties, which seemed appropriately old for a grandparent when I was eight, but shockingly young now that I'm chasing that age myself.

One morning, my grandmother's research assistant arrived wearing loose jeans and a blouse, lugging a legal box full of paperwork, blonde hair knotted up on top of her head and sunglasses sliding down the end of her nose. Beverly was an English major at Angelo State with an eye toward folklore and the supernatural, and her whirlwind arrival blew the ghosts to hidden corners of the house. I'd learned the summer before that despite her interest in ghosts, Beverly couldn't see the ones living here. She struck me as too energetic, too *alive* for the ghosts to reveal themselves.

I wasn't sure what that said about me.

"Hey kid, what are you reading?" Beverly sat the box on the table and gave me a hug. I showed her the paperback in my hand. "I like that one," she said. "But I like his science fiction stuff better."

My grandmother greeted Beverly wearing an orange polyester pantsuit and the wig she wore whenever we left the house, or when company called. She dug through the papers Beverly had brought, turquoise bracelets clattering together on her wrists. She clenched a lit cigarette between her teeth when she spoke. "Any accounts here from primary sources?"

Beverly settled into a chair at the dining room table, where my grandmother had already spilled the paperwork across the surface in untidy stacks. "Not much. Nothing that would be new to you, anyway. But there's some good general info about the time period, and a lot of quotable speculation over the years of what CROATOAN might mean."

"Thank you, honey. Looks like some good stuff."

"I also found some stories I don't think you've referenced yet that might add color and corroboration. Small towns in California and Ohio that disappeared around the turn of the century. And this one here in Kansas, back in the fifties."

Beverly slid a paper-clipped bundle of materials toward my grandmother.

"You're talking about Ashley, Kansas?"

"Yes. Earthquake, fire from the sky. A lot of creepy calls to the cops about the dead coming back for a visit. And then everybody in the whole town just disappeared. There are a couple of phone numbers written down there. People who lived nearby when it happened. I got a hold of them, and they're willing to talk to you."

"This is good work. I've heard that story before, but nothing as detailed as this."

"There's talk of a hole in the sky," said Beverly. "Maybe it connects to another dimension? That supports a scientific answer to this mystery, don't you think?"

"Might be it does," said my grandmother. "Either way, it's interesting."

I huddled underneath the table like one of the ghosts, hungry for scraps. I often learned more about what Beverly and my grandmother were researching when they forgot I was there. Shirley attached herself to the underside of the table too, a swirling mass with shining eyes, head cocked to the side like she was listening. We lazed there together, lulled half asleep by the heat and their voices.

"Another universe bumping up against this one is the only rational explanation, isn't it?" Beverly took a seat at the table and tapped her shoe nervously against the floorboards. Shirley drifted close, grasped at the cuff of Beverly's blue jeans with smoky fingers. Shirley had that dusty, moldering smell that many of us associate with long afternoons spent digging through forgotten bookstores, and I would carry that with me through life as the scent of my grandmother's house.

"Why do you assume there's a rational explanation?" my grandmother asked.

"There has to be, right?"

"There has to be an explanation," my grandmother said, "but no reason it has to be rational."

Granny wrote nonfiction books about the supernatural, and her latest project was about the Roanoke colony. I'd read about what happened there. As soon as I was old enough to sound out words, my grandmother loaded me down with books about aliens, bigfoot, ghosts, trolls living under bridges, portals to fairy kingdoms, doomsday cults, and by comparison, more prosaic mysteries like the story of Roanoke. I knew Roanoke was a colony of early American settlers who had disappeared in the late fifteen hundreds, leaving no clue to where they'd gone, except the word CROATOAN cut into the bark of a tree. Most historians figured they'd either been killed by natives or assimilated into one of their tribes, but such an enduring mystery was bound to elicit supernatural speculation as well.

I peered out from underneath the table, spying on them like another forgotten ghost.

"If you throw out science, how can you hope to figure all this out?" said Beverly. "That's crazy, right?"

Before Granny moved here, before she got *sick*, she taught high school. English 101. Both levels of Spanish. She was accustomed to questions and reveled in learning. So, she accepted Beverly's challenge in the spirit it was intended.

Granny smiled, struggled with the striker on her lighter as she started another cigarette.

"I don't throw out science, honey," she said. "And I don't doubt there's some *rational* outcome for what's going on that you'd accept in those terms, if you had a textbook in your hands that codified it. But that won't ever happen. Science won't provide you that answer. You know why? Science is too *proud*. Science won't dig deep enough. I've read reams of evidence on the supernatural, including your good work here. Testimonials by credible folks with no reason to lie. Photos. Recordings. Objectively provable psychic phenomena. Do scientists consider these things? Not many of them. Not if they value their reputation. No quicker way to get shunned by academia than admit you believe in ghosts and goblins. And that's a shame. Because science is supposed to consider *all* evidence, isn't it? How accurate can your finding be on a matter if you pretend a good bulk of evidence just doesn't exist?"

"I don't know," said Beverly.

"Well, they don't either. What I'm saying, girl, is all that stuff we call the supernatural is a *natural* part of science. You just can't study it under a microscope or swirl it around in a test tube."

"You know I love folklore," said Beverly. "*Stories*. But there must be some real-world answer for these sorts of disappearances, right? These people aren't being stolen away by fairies."

"You're sure of that?"

Beverly grinned, chewed at her bottom lip as she tried to figure out if Granny was joking. Tried to ready some sort of logical argument if she wasn't. The genuine delight on her face, and the way she drew her hair back through her fingers when she was thinking intently, made something flutter in my stomach. She smelled like coconut shampoo and sunshine. Like she lived on a tropical beach and not in the same forsaken land as the rest of us. Beverly belonged someplace else. Someplace better. She was beautiful, and I suppose I had a crush on her, but my eight-year-old self wouldn't have understood it in those terms.

"You know I've experienced things too?" said Granny. "Not to mention there's ghosts all over this house. Brady here sees them. Don't you?"

Blood rushed to my face, and I nodded. Beverly gave me an appraising look, like she wasn't sure what planet I'd materialized from.

"You've told me all the stories, Mrs. Edwards."

"They're more than *stories*," said Granny.

"Sorry, that's not what I meant. I believe all this stuff is happening, but there's just..." Beverly trailed off, absently flipped through a few of the pages on the tabletop, as if the secrets of the universe might suddenly reveal themselves.

"Uh huh," said Granny. "That's where we get caught up, isn't it? *Just*. That's where our strictly materialist view of the universe falls apart."

"I just need something to hold on to," said Beverly.

"That's the trick, ain't it?"

Shirley drifted from underneath the table like silver smoke, her swirling surface capturing sunlight from another world. Her smile was mischief, and her eyes burned blue. She wanted me to follow. Shirley was restless; she never liked to remain in one place for long unless she was listening to me read. Books always calmed her. Rooted her in the world. I was the same way. I could burn away long hours without moving, so long as there were other places for me to visit in the pages of a book.

Never squirming, never impatient.

Other places always seemed better than wherever I was.

The flavor of conversation between Granny and Beverly was the same as always, so when Shirley issued the call to adventure, I followed. Crawled on all fours like a coyote sniffing at her trail. She moved across the kitchen linoleum like fog creeping across the face of the world, escaped the room and advanced down the hallway. Moving, eventually, under the closed door that led into Granny's den. My bare hands and feet slapped against the floorboards as I followed. The wood was stained with something dark, and smelled like animals had lived here long ago.

A ghost I'd named Glen waited at the doorway. Might be he was standing guard, but I couldn't know his motives. I wasn't allowed in Granny's den alone. But I was determined to follow Shirley, find out what she was up to. Glen was the ghost of an old cowboy with a crushed and weathered hat; he was nothing but bones inside his musty suit. Sometimes he wore a drawn, fretful face, wrinkled and ashen, but today he revealed only his gray, pitted skull, half his teeth fallen out and cracks radiating out from one eye socket like rays from the noonday sun. Shadows ruled the hallway, and he drew form from the darkness, appearing almost substantial. His jaw opened and closed with a sound like a cinder block dragging over concrete. Whatever he wanted to say, I wasn't listening. I reached through him, turned the glass-handled doorknob, and proceeded into the den.

The room Granny called her *den* was a study, just off the hallway near the front entrance to the house. A cracked brick fireplace dominated one wall, mouth black and choking out the old scent of mesquite ash. Bookshelves crowded the other walls, overflowing with titles like *The Kybalion. The Secret Teachings of All Ages. The Book of Lies.* All manner of seductive-sounding volumes that drew my young self in like bugs to the porch lights. I had free run of Granny's bookshelves, apart from those in her den. I would not read these books until much later, when I was older, and seeking insight into my grandmother's thinking, there at the end of her life. I can't say it made much of a difference.

Questing for any true answer was folly, though it took me decades to learn that.

Stuffed in with the books were file folders and yellow notebooks full of Granny's neat handwriting. Stacks of generic white cassette tapes with labels like *Little Girl Ghost, Jumping on Bed. Snyder, TX 1972* and *Interview #2 with Mrs. Mabel Starch / Plainview Prairie Beast Encounter.* Melted candles and grinning crystal skulls. Wooden boxes carved with smiling suns and sleeping moons. Shirley rested a hand on top of one of those boxes, smiling dreamily. Her intention clear. Summer sunlight tried to intrude through the room's lone window, but tan lace curtains and layers of West Texas dust held it at bay. What light existed in the room was golden and soft. *Ghost light.* Perfect shading for Shirley to take form. Unseen winds pulled at her calico dress. Her fingers clutched at the box, like she was trying to lift it herself. I didn't question her. I met her hopeful stare and nodded. Snatched the box from the shelf and held it in my tiny hands.

I climbed into the swivel chair at Granny's big oak desk, sat the box on top, careful not to disturb anything. Not to leave evidence of my *trespass.* The desk was littered with scraps of paper, mostly letters from people who sought out my grandmother for her advice on the supernatural. A few photos lay scattered about. Blurry images of supposed ghosts, and one that looked like a canine jowl streaking red through thick sagebrush. That one was paper clipped to a handwritten note claiming an encounter with the Chupacabra.

Normally these photos would have drawn me in; they weren't among those Granny had shown me before. But the wooden box held the promise of unknown treasure, and Shirley clung cold against my back, obviously eager for me to open it. When I did, I found more photos. A couple dozen of them, bound in a fat rubber band. Every one of them taken inside Granny's house. I heard that cinder-block scrape again, and realized Glen had joined us. He stood right behind me, snared by the same curiosity that held Shirley. The same curiosity that held me.

I fumbled off the rubber band. Laid the photos out.

The shooting locations were instantly recognizable. Granny's upstairs bedroom. The kitchen, in the corner where the wobbly breakfast table stood. The formal living room, in front of the great brick fireplace. Even a few in the bathroom. Every photo taken right here in Granny's house; every photo filled with ghostly apparitions. None of the ghosts appeared on film as clearly as they did to my waking eyes, but a few were substantial enough that I recognized them as my friends. One photo captured the old woman I'd named Lady Pecan Tree, standing beside the bed in my room, staring out the dormer window as was her habit. Blue and shimmery and transparent. Another photo showed Glen in the front living room, worn hat tipped forward to cover most of his missing face. Ephemeral hands locked together in worry. I kept flipping through the photos, found one of myself, very much alive, standing in front the towering bookshelves in the library. Some of the photos were older, but Granny took this one. Shirley stood beside me, both of us staring at the camera, like we were posing together. And I suppose we were. Shirley and I were fast friends, no matter the distance that separated us. No matter how much she wished me dead, so we might play and read together for eternity.

The ghosts at my back remained cold and still.

None of these photos were remotely frightening, and as I continued to examine them, I wondered why Granny held this particular batch in reserve.

Then I came to the last photo in the pile.

It was taken in the entryway, the camera eye facing the front door. A stained glass window dominated the top half of the door; it showed a stylized reproduction of an old-time cattle drive, beeves lumbering across the vanished prairie, cowboys on horseback, herding them ever onward. Sunlight stampeded through the glass, spilling reds and greens and golds across the floor and the walls. Bathed in that sunlight was the ghost of a man, arms crossed and grinning. So striking was the image, that if not for the way the sunlight passed through him, I might have mistaken him for a visitor to the house, waiting by the door to leave. He wore a pair of green coveralls, pants legs tucked into tall boots. His gray hair was thin and neatly combed, and a few days' worth of stubble grew on his chin. His green eyes shone with otherworldly light. They stared at the camera. Stared at the photographer. Stared at *me.*

It was my grandfather.

Five years dead.

Granny, it seemed, had good reason for her secrets.

———————————

Summer in the House of the Departed
by Josh Rountree
Coming from Psychopomp, Summer 2025

Join our mailing list to stay up to date on this and other exciting releases, psychopomp.com

Josh Rountree is a Texas novelist and short story writer. His novel, *The Legend of Charlie Fish*, was released by Tachyon Publications in 2023 to wide acclaim, making the Locus Recommended Reading List, and being named one of Los Angeles Public Library's best books of the year. A followup novel, *The Unkillable Frank Lightning*, was published in the summer of 2025. More than seventy of his short stories have been published in a variety of venues, including *The Deadlands, Beneath Ceaseless Skies, Bourbon Penn, Realms of Fantasy, PseudoPod, Weird Horror,* and *The Year's Best Dark Fantasy & Horror*. Several collections of his short fiction have been published, including *Fantastic Americana,* and most recently, *Death Aesthetic,* featuring tales of death and transformation. Rountree lives in Austin with his lovely wife of many years, and a pair of half-feral dogs who demand his obedience.